ONE NATION UNDER GOD

RUDY CAIN   TURNER BEALL

Published by
World Video Bible School®
25 Lantana Lane
Maxwell, Texas 78656
www.wvbs.org

ISBN: 978-0-9967003-8-2

Cover art by Aubrie Deaver

Layout by Aubrie Deaver

wvbs.org

The Story:
This fictional story is by Rudy Cain.
May God receive the glory.

Special thanks to:
Aubrie Deaver and her work in transcribing
the story from oral words to printed page.

The Book:
Developed by Elizabeth Turner Beall

This story is dedicated to:
The Lord's Church around the world.

**Special thanks to those who proofed
and helped with this book:**
Glenn Beall
Lacey Deaver
Sharon Cain
Rachel Howard
Loretta Horner

Disclaimer:
This is a work of fiction. Names, characters, businesses, places, locales, and events are the products of the authors' imagination or used in a fictitious manner. Any resemblance to actual persons, living or dead, or actual events is purely coincidental.

TABLE OF CONTENTS

CHAPTER 1

THE STORM

A thin, clean-shaven Chinese man in his mid-thirties stood at the hotel front desk where he had just checked out. Beside him stood an attractive, delicate-looking Chinese woman in her late twenties, her hair pulled away from her face and held back with an ivory comb. Both were dressed business casual. As they turned to leave, a large, flat-screen TV on the opposite wall of the lobby caught his attention. The weatherman was showing viewers a large weather pattern off the coast of Oregon as he spoke.

"This winter storm is coming in from the Bering Sea with a lot of moisture. It's predicted to be one of the worst we've seen in a while with severe blizzard conditions in the higher elevations from Barstow, California to Mt. Saint Helens. The storm will have high winds and heavy snow, especially in the mountains. Blizzard warnings are out for the Cascades in Oregon, and south through the Sierra Nevada mountains in California. The storm will continue to push east and should reach the Denver area in less than two days."

The Chinese man studied the map a bit more, then said to the woman in Chinese, "We must go. We have to get through the mountains and into San Francisco before the storm hits."

In their car the man looked at his phone's map app, confirming to himself that from Cheyenne, Wyoming, they would need to go west on US 80 to Salt Lake City, then to Reno, Nevada.

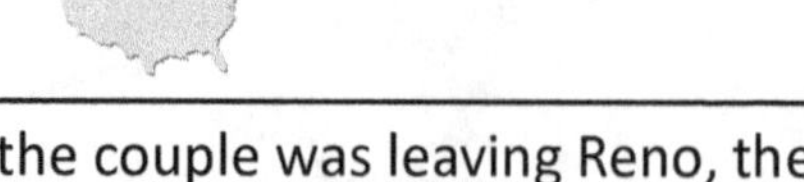

Two days later, as the couple was leaving Reno, the snowfall grew worse and the woman said, "It is snowing hard. Should we go back to town?"

"No. We must be in San Francisco tomorrow. We can get through these mountains in a couple of hours and when we are out of the mountains, we will be out of the snow." He looked at the woman and said, "We must hurry and get through this."

It was almost 4 p.m. when they went through Truckee Crossing near Donner Pass, but seemed much later because of the heavy snowfall. Wind gusts up to 60 miles an hour made the snowfall appear heavier. More and more vehicles pulled off the highway onto the emergency lanes. Thinking they would be through the storm soon, the man pressed on down the road, even though he couldn't see more than one car length ahead. A few minutes later, the highway curved sharply, but he mistakenly continued straight onto a road headed away from where they needed to go. The man soon realized he was no longer on an interstate, but a small mountain roadway.

The snow fell heavier and faster, whipped around by the fierce winds. Suddenly the roadway took a steep decline, taking the car with it towards the bottom of a deep canyon. Immediately they were both concerned. Not only were they on the wrong road, there was no place to turn around.

As the car began the steep downhill run mixed with the snow and the strong wind, all control of the car was lost. The car careened from one side of the road to the other. Moving faster and faster down the mountain, it crashed against large boulders and tree limbs along the side of the road. There was nothing the couple could do but hang on, he to the steering wheel with a white-knuckled grip, and she with both hands clinging to the seatbelt crossed over her body. They were terrified by the speed of the car and the sound of rocks and tree limbs hitting against its sides. Suddenly they hit a large embankment. The airbags deployed and filled the front seats as they exploded. The car veered off the edge of the road, entangled in three large trees, and came to an abrupt stop.

Seconds passed as the couple tried to regain their composure from the frightening ordeal they had just been through. From his side of the car, the man called out to the woman, "Are you alright?"

"I think so," she said, not completely sure. Then she asked the man, "Are you alright?" When she pushed the airbags away, she cried out at what she saw. A tree limb had come through the windshield and had driven into the man's right side just above his lung near his shoulder. To her it looked deep as it pinned him tightly against the seat so he could not move his body.

She started to put her hand on the limb, but the man quickly said, "Do not touch it."

Tears filled her eyes as she asked, "What are we going to do?"

The man realized the car was not running and probably would not start, which also meant there would be no heat to keep them warm. He again took notice of the hard-falling snow and fierce wind, and understood there would only be a short time left in the freezing weather. Even if he could get free, there was no place to go. He looked over at her and said, "I believe we will die here."

The woman bent over with her face in her hands and began to sob. A few minutes later, she sat up again and leaned back against the seat with a resigned stare. The inside of the car was cold.

"I saw a light!" the woman cried out. The man looked about but saw nothing. "It was on for just a few seconds, but I saw it. I am sure I saw it! It was just ahead and to the left," she said. Quickly she got out of the car without thought to test her footing. She headed down towards where she believed she had seen the light. After she had struggled about fifty yards through the snow, she was able to see other lights from windows,

and made her way to some kind of building. The woman was exhausted by the time she reached the house. Pounding on the door, she knew the howling wind was louder than any noise she could make. It seemed forever before the flood light she had seen earlier lit up the area around the front of the house.

Someone unlocked the door and cracked it open. A woman's voice asked, "Who are you?"

In simple English, the woman outside begged, "Help me! Help me, please!"

The door quickly opened and the woman inside grabbed the Chinese woman by the arm, pulling her into the warmth of the cabin. Closing the door hard, the woman turned to the Chinese lady and asked, "How did you get here? Where are you from? How did you survive out there?"

The delicate woman tried to get her wits about her and think clearly. Again, in her limited English, she managed to say, "The car wrecked. Man is hurt. He will die. Help us please."

At that moment, an unshaven man with graying brown hair came out of another room with a blanket wrapped around him. Coughing and sniffling, he asked, "What's going on?"

The man's wife said, "There's apparently been a car wreck nearby and there's a man who's badly hurt."

The man hesitated a moment, then said, "I'll get dressed and go after him. Get Kasey. Tell him I'll need his help."

Standing at the top of the stairway were two brown-haired teenagers, a boy about seventeen and a girl about fifteen. "Dad, I'll get ready," the boy said and disappeared into an unseen room.

The blonde-headed woman walked over to her husband and said, "Brad, you can't go out there. You still have a fever. You'll kill yourself! And Kasey's still recovering. It's too risky for either one of you to go outside. As sick as we've all been, none of us needs to be out in this." She paused. "And besides, you don't have enough strength to go fifty feet in that snow."

Brad paused, covered his wife's hand with his, and said, "Carol, if we don't try to help him, he will die out there for sure."

When Brad went back into the room to get dressed, Carol brought the Chinese woman over to the fireplace and sat her down in a chair to warm up. Then she scurried about the house gathering up rubber boots, coats, scarves, and hats that had been packed away before they had all taken sick.

Brad returned to the room and asked the Chinese woman, "In what direction is the wreck?" She pointed at an angle to the door, hoping it was the direction she had come.

Brad sat down to pull his boots on. His son came over and said, "I'm ready to go, Dad."

Brad instructed, "Son, go to the storage area and get the big sled there."

Soon the two men were ready to go out the door. Each one had a flashlight and blankets. Brad switched on the flood light and looked out the window. Snow was still falling hard and the wind was whipping through the trees. For a moment he thought to himself, *This is crazy. I can't do this.*

His wife voiced his thoughts, "Brad, you cannot do this. You are risking your life and the life of your son if you go out there."

"The man needs help," Brad replied without hesitation. "No one else can do that but us. We must go."

From across the room the Chinese woman watched and listened, shaking with cold and fear, as she thought how risky this was going to be.

The two men went out the door. Carol closed it and leaned against it briefly. She walked over to the table and sat down, clasped her hands together, and leaned her head on her hands. Softly, but audibly, she began to pray.

The Chinese lady looked around, not knowing what to do. Never before had she seen or heard anything like this.

It seemed forever before Brad and his son reached the car, almost missing it in the snowdrift. Brad swiped the snow away, yanked open the car door, and gasped. "Oh man! This looks bad." He took a deep breath, held it a few seconds, then exhaled slowly. "Kasey, get in the back seat of the car."

As Kasey squirmed to get into the back seat, he spied the limb in the man's chest. It looked almost two feet long and a couple of inches thick. "Dad?" Kasey said, filling that one word with unspoken questions.

"He's still alive but freezing. We have to hurry," his father said. When Brad grabbed the man's arm, he opened his eyes and looked directly at Brad. "It's ok. We're going to help you," Brad assured him.

The man nodded slightly, grimaced, and whispered, "Thank you," then closed his eyes.

Brad said to his son, "The limb broke off at the window and if the limb comes out of him, he could start bleeding and will be dead before we get him home. I want you to hold the limb and keep it pressed tightly against him so it doesn't come out." Kasey positioned himself and placed both hands on the limb. Brad said, "I'm going to lay him and the seat back to take pressure off the limb. Then I'm going to drag him out onto the sled." Brad gave Kasey a quick look and said, "You're going to have to do all you can to keep that limb in and upright."

As Brad laid the driver's seat back, releasing the pressure, the limb came free from the window. When Brad laid him down, the man let out a painful moan and passed out. Brad said aloud, "Good. If he's unconscious, it will make the trip easier."

Brad began to drag the man out of the car onto the sled,

but suddenly realized that all of the adrenaline he had used was now gone. He felt weak and could only think of lying down in the snow, not moving his arms or legs. His body simply had nothing left. He began to repeat to himself over and over in his mind, *God, please get us all home. Please, Father, help us.*

With all the blankets on the man and Kasey holding the limb upright, Brad began pulling the sled. He could see the flood light on the house three hundred feet away. He tried to stay in the path because he knew it would be the easiest way back. It took every ounce of strength in him to keep putting one foot in front of the other. The trip back to the house felt much longer, and when they arrived at the door, Brad didn't even have the strength to knock or yell. He simply fell against it with a hard thud.

The door opened and the women dragged Brad and the man on the sled into the house and across the floor next to the large fireplace. Carol and the Chinese woman placed blankets over each man. A couple of blankets also went to Kasey, who now had his knees against the man, holding onto the limb as best he could.

Carol grabbed Brad's wrists. "His pulse is very weak," she said softly. She turned and took the stranger's wrist. A few seconds passed. She shook her head and said, "His is even worse."

Carol shouted, "We must get them warm or they're going to die!" Carol took wet towels she had earlier put on the fireplace hearth, and barked out orders to her daughter and the Chinese woman. "Roll up their pant legs and shirt sleeves and rub them with the towels."

As they followed her instructions, Carol opened each man's jacket and shirt, and placed a large, warm, wet towel on each man's chest to heat up his body. Carol spoke again, "We must get them conscious so they can drink something hot."

Several minutes passed before Brad came around and was able to sit up and lean against the couch. Bailey handed her

dad a cup of hot tea and sat a cup of hot soup beside him on the floor.

Carol and the other woman continued working on the Chinese man, rubbing his arms and legs with warm, wet, towels. Carol tied the limb so it no longer needed to be held by Kasey, who now sat on the edge of the fireplace hearth also drinking hot tea and eating soup.

Carol looked at the Chinese woman and said, "I'm sorry. I didn't get your name."

"I am Meili, but in English I am Mary," the woman responded softly, her beautiful eyes still fearful in her delicate face.

Carol smiled at her and said, "I'm Carol." Both women looked at each other for a moment. Carol asked, "What is his name?"

"Ungan."

"Ungan," Carol repeated, then turned toward him, and with one swoop she slapped him across the face as she called out in a loud voice, "Ungan! Wake up! We need you here!" Everyone in the room sat up, startled.

"In English his name is John," Mary said, not sure what to make of Carol's actions.

Again, Carol hit him on the other side of the face and yelled out, "Come on, John! We need you here, now! Wake up!"

John's legs trembled and his head shook as he slowly regained consciousness. Within a few seconds he opened his eyes and looked around, first at the two women, then at the limb still sticking out of his body. Looking at Mary, he asked in Chinese, "Where are we?"

"In the home of these people," Mary replied softly.

"Have I been out long?" he questioned again.

"Maybe an hour."

Suddenly Carol interrupted, "Can you speak English?"

He looked at her and answered, "Yes."

Carol continued, "We need to set you up so you can drink some hot tea and soup."

"Okay," he agreed, and the two women placed their hands under each shoulder to help lift him slightly so he was almost sitting up. He groaned and grimaced, but managed to remain conscious. Kasey slid a chair over to help hold him in his propped-up position.

After a cup of tea and small bowl of soup, he seemed to be doing better, except for the limb protruding from his chest. John looked at Brad, who was still sitting on the floor eating soup.

John asked, "Can an ambulance take me to the hospital?"

"I'm sorry," Brad replied, "there is no way to drive in or out of here."

"Can you call for some help?"

"Sorry," Brad replied again. "There's no cell phone service here in the canyon."

Brad turned, looked at Carol, and raised an eyebrow in a silent question.

Carol shook her head so hard her shoulder-length hair fell over her face. "I can't do that," she said.

"You must," Brad replied.

"I have no anesthetic, no antibiotics, and no sutures."

John looked from one to the other as they spoke.

"We have no other choice. You have to do it," Brad said firmly.

John frowned with concern and asked, "Do what?"

"My wife used to be a surgical nurse. She's going to have to take that tree out of your chest, and soon before it gets infected."

John looked at Carol. Their eyes locked briefly before Carol replied, "Brad is right. That's going to have to come out soon."

"But can you do it?"

"I don't want to... but I can," Carol admitted.

John sat deep in thought wondering what he should do.

Mary spoke up in Chinese, "I am afraid. What are you going to do?"

"I have no choice. I have to let her take it out." John looked at Carol again. "You can do it?"

"I guess I'll have to."

Carol hurried about the house gathering up things needed for the impromptu procedure. She stopped and asked Mary, "Can you see blood and not get sick?"

"I can do alright," Mary replied.

"Good. Then go wash your hands with soap and hot water three times, and touch nothing afterwards."

Carol turned to her daughter. "Get a white sheet, and you and your dad cut some long strips about a quarter of an inch wide. Then put them in a pot of boiling water on the stove."

Carol turned to her son. "Get the sharpest knife from the kitchen with a wooden handle. Get a pan and fill it half full with hot coals from the fireplace."

When Carol had everything she needed, Brad and Kasey helped John to his feet and into the guest bedroom. After laying him on the bed, Carol sat down in the chair beside him and said, "Sorry, John, but your arms and legs have to be tied down. If you were to try and hit me, we would both be in trouble."

Brad and Kasey stepped back from tying John down. Carol asked, "Are you ready?"

John looked worried and asked, "Nothing for pain? No whiskey?"

"Sorry," Carol answered softly. "We don't have anything in the house like that." Carol looked around the room and asked, "Are you ready?" At their nods, she took a plastic spatula handle, placed it between John's teeth, and said, "You'll just have to bite down as you need to."

Kasey again held the limb. Carol directed, "Slowly start to pull it up and out of him." The limb began to move. John bit down hard, let out a loud painful moan, and passed out. "It's better this way," Carol said to the others in the room.

"Mary, help me now," Carol said. As she had been shown earlier, Mary placed two fingers of each hand into the wound and pulled it open as wide as she could. Bailey held a bright light over the hole so Carol could see into it. With tweezers, Carol removed wood fragments from the wound. When she had cleaned it out, she took the hot knife from the coals and cauterized two or three places where blood was seeping in from small blood vessels.

Carol picked up a bottle of 100% alcohol and said, "Untie his left arm. With no antibiotics, this is all I can do to disinfect it." She poured the whole bottle into the wound until it was running over. "Turn him on his side and let the alcohol run out." They turned him, let the alcohol empty out, then returned him to his back and re-tied his arm.

Carol picked up the tweezers and removed the boiled strips of sheets from the pot one by one. She shook each one

briefly in the air to cool, then packed them into the wound until it was full. To complete her work, she placed a gauze bandage over the wound, then tied and taped his right arm to his body so he could not move it.

"Well," Carol said, "That's all we can do except pray for him. He needs to rest now as best he can. Someone needs to stay here and keep watch over him. Come get me when he regains consciousness."

"I will stay with him here," Mary said.

"Good. I'll be on the couch if you need me," Carol said. Everyone else went to bed.

CHAPTER 2

THE RECOVERY

Everyone slept in from the long, trying night. Late the next morning Carol and her daughter prepared food; the smell of coffee and bacon filled the house. Carol went into the guest bedroom to check on John. Mary had slept in the chair, but woke up as Carol came in.

Carol checked John's pulse, took his temperature, and lifted the bandage to examine the wound. She motioned Mary to follow her out of the room. Outside the door, Carol said, "He has a good pulse, no fever, and the wound looks good. I think he is past the worst of it and will probably come around in a few hours."

Mary placed her hands on her face with a smile of joy and said, "Thank you for what you have done for John."

"I'm just thankful that God has given John his life," Carol said. "Come, let's get you some breakfast." Mary smiled, said "Thank you," and followed Carol into the kitchen.

After Mary finished eating, Carol brought in some clothes of her own so Mary could clean up. When Mary returned to the guest bedroom, Brad was sitting in the chair next to the bed, softly praying for John. She wasn't sure what to do, but quietly entered the room and stood on the other side of the bed.

Brad completed his prayer. He looked up and smiled at Mary. "If it is God's will, John will be alright." Brad then got up

and left the room.

Throughout the day, Carol checked John's vital signs every half hour. About 2 o'clock in the afternoon Mary called out to Carol, "John is moving about!" Everyone in the house hurried into the room to see how John was doing.

His eyes were now open as Carol checked his pulse once more and asked, "How are you feeling?"

John spoke in Chinese and Mary translated. "He said he is glad to be alive."

Brad and Carol stood next to each other beside the bed, holding hands. Carol spoke first. "Thanks be to God that you are back with us."

"The Lord has blessed you to get you through this ordeal and thanks be to Him," Brad added.

"Let's set you up a little so you can eat something," Carol suggested.

Mary stood on the other side of the bed across from Carol. Both women reached under each arm and slid John into a somewhat upright position. Mary smiled and left the room.

Carol looked at the wound again and said, "John, you are truly blessed that the limb was stopped from going deeper by your pectoral muscle. And because it was stuck in the muscle, there wasn't a lot of bleeding." She paused then added, "There's no infection around the wound now and no temperature. We will pray that no infection occurs before we can get you to a doctor."

John looked at Carol and asked, "How can I ever thank you?"

Carol smiled, a little embarrassed. "Don't thank me. Thank God. It's He Who watched over you."

Mary came into the room with a tray of food.

"I'll leave you two alone," Carol said. "Call me if you need me."

When they were alone they spoke in Chinese. "While I was unconscious, did I say anything?" John asked with concern in his voice.

"No. Not at all," Mary assured him.

"What kind of people are these?" John asked.

"They seem very nice." Mary paused. "They pray a lot, especially before they eat, and I heard them praying for you and your health. I also saw the man here at your bedside praying for you." She hesitated then asked, "Do you think they are Jews?"

John said, "I don't know. Did you see any statues of gods around the house?"

"No. None," Mary replied. After a few seconds in thought she continued. "They are good to each other. They seem willing to help us in any way they can. The man and the boy risked their own lives to go and get you from the car."

At that moment, Carol stopped at the open door and smiled. "In a little while you need to get up and start walking around the house."

About 6 p.m. that evening, Carol came to the guest bedroom door and knocked. When Mary came to the door, Carol said, "We'll be eating in about 10 minutes." She hesitated a moment. "Since John walked around a couple of times this afternoon, perhaps he'll be able to join us for dinner?"

Mary looked into the room at John, then turned back to Carol and smiled. "Yes, we will be glad to join you."

At the dinner table, Brad said, "Let's give thanks." He bowed his head with his family and offered a prayer of thanksgiving for John's continued improvement, and for the food they were going to eat.

As Brad prayed, John and Mary looked at those who sat with bowed heads and closed eyes, then at each other as if they did not understand what "giving thanks" was all about.

After the food was passed around the table, John asked Brad, "Do you have any idea when help might come?"

"Well, I think the storm has passed. If the snow stops tonight, and the sun comes out tomorrow, and the temperatures go up, I believe Kasey and I can hike out of the canyon and up to the highway. Maybe three days from now. But if it stays cold and overcast, it may be more than a week." Brad looked at Carol and asked, "What does our food supply look like? Will it hold up for several days for all of us?"

Carol smiled, looked at Kasey and said, "It all depends on Kasey. He eats everything he sees. You know how boys his age are."

Kasey spoke up. "I can go hunting and kill something for us to eat."

Brad said, "Son, there's nothing moving out there in that deep snow. Even if it warms up, it would take days for the snow to melt down before you could even think of going hunting."

It grew quiet around the table as everyone ate. After a few minutes John questioned Brad again. "Would there be any way to get the bags out of the car to the house?"

Brad looked at Kasey and asked, "What do you think? Would you say the car is a hundred yards or so from the house?"

"I think so. I could go that far tomorrow."

"Son, let's see what the weather's like. If the snow stops, maybe you can shovel a path from the house to the road. Then we'll be able to see what we can do."

John looked at both men and replied, "Thank you for

your help."

After dinner Kasey put more wood on the fire. Carol and her daughter set out candles in every bedroom. Once the candles were lit, Brad turned off the generator for the night to save gas. Good-nights were said and everyone went to their rooms.

The next morning Carol was up first and put on the coffee. When she went into the living room, she found Mary on the couch wrapped in blankets. Carol studied her a moment, then mumbled softly, "She doesn't look well. It's probably the flu. I sure hope John doesn't come down with it. It's nasty."

After the coffee was made, Carol walked to the bottom of the stairway and called up, "Kasey, come down and add wood to the fireplace, please."

Later, while Brad and Carol drank coffee in the kitchen and talked about what needed to be done that day, Kasey came by the kitchen on his way back to bed.

"Son, how's our wood supply?" Brad asked.

"It's really good," Kasey assured him. "The wood man must've left two cords and we have at least one and a half left."

"Good," Brad said. "Would you check on how much propane is in the tank? Also find out how much gas is in the SUV in case we need it for the generator."

"Yes sir," Kasey responded. "Can you give me about an hour? I'm still sleepy."

"Sure," Brad said.

"Great, Dad," Kasey said as he turned to go, and met John at the door. "Good morning, sir," Kasey greeted.

"Good morning," John said automatically. He looked at Brad, then at Carol, and then at the empty chair.

"Mary's in the living room on the couch," Carol said, knowing who John was looking for. "She looks like she has the flu. I took her temperature a few minutes ago and it's 101 degrees. She isn't feeling well at all. Let's hope you don't get it." She stood up. "Can I get you a cup of coffee?"

"Yes, thank you," John said. "I will go and check on Mary first."

"How are you feeling today?" Carol asked John when he returned to the kitchen.

"I am okay, but my shoulder hurt a lot during the night."

"I don't have anything except that big bottle of aspirin," Carol said as she turned to Brad. "Would you get John some aspirin while I get his breakfast?"

When Brad left the room, Carol asked John, "Would eggs and toast be okay for breakfast?"

"Yes, thank you," he said, and sat down at the table.

Brad returned with the aspirin and poured out four on the table where John sat. "Thank you," John said. He sat silent a moment, took a deep breath, then spoke again. "I must thank you again, Brad, for risking your life, and your son's life, to come and get me out of the car. I know I would have died if you had not helped me. And Carol, you saved my life by operating on me. How can I repay you for all that you have done?"

"There is no pay," Brad said. "We only did what God would have us do. We always need to help our neighbor as we have opportunity. My family and I were glad to be able to help you and Mary in your time of need."

Carol continued when Brad took a breath. "The Lord teaches us to do good to all people and to love our neighbor as ourselves. It was simply the right thing to do."

"Yes," Brad said. "The Lord expects us to be of help to anyone who is in need, if we can. Thank God we were here."

Carol spoke up. "We were going to leave ahead of the storm, except we all got so sick from the flu that we couldn't leave."

John broke in, "I, too, am very glad you were here, because if you had not been here, Mary and I would surely have died."

Brad said, "We can never know how God's providence works, but we can be glad that we were able to help."

John looked at the two of them and said, "You both are good people."

At that moment, Kasey returned to the kitchen. "Mom, I'm going to need a big breakfast so I can start digging out the snow."

"Now son," Brad spoke up. "You need to be careful out there. The snow is high near the house and on the roof and it could fall on you. I want your sister to sit at the window and watch you in case something happens."

Carol took her turn. "And don't overdo it. You don't need to get sick again."

Kasey walked over to Carol, put his arm around her shoulders and said with a big grin, "I'll be careful, Mom, but I'll still need that big breakfast first."

Two hours later, Brad sat in one of the two over-stuffed chairs facing the large bay window that overlooked the canyon floor. Today that floor was covered in a deep blanket of snow. Brad sat in the glow of the morning sun that streamed through the window, warming him and much of the room around him. His Bible lay open on his lap.

John walked around the room and slowly made his way to the other big chair next to Brad. When John sat down, Brad closed the Bible and placed it on the table between the two chairs. "How are you feeling?"

"I am feeling much better. I will be back to my old self soon. Carol wanted me to sit in the sun for a while." John smiled as he looked out the window. It was a nice, warm place to sit.

"Good news," Brad said. "We do have a break in the weather and the sun is out, as you can see. And if the sun stays out for a few days, we could get out of here sooner than I thought."

John smiled. "That will be good," he said as he looked over at Brad. "May I ask you a question?"

"Sure." Brad settled deeper into the chair, keeping eye contact with John.

"Mary told me she saw you by my bed praying for me. We wondered if you are Jews."

Brad smiled. "No, we're not. What made you think we're Jews?"

"I had been told there were many Jews in America, and that America was a defender of Israel because they were God's people."

"Well, God's history tells us that about 4,000 years ago God did single out and make a nation of people that He called His own. After about 2,000 years, God sent His only Son to help His people as well as all the people of the world. God, through His Son, made promises to all the people and established a way that any and all people who accepted His Son as their King and religious leader would receive God's new promises. Any people who rejected His Son and would not believe in Him and His authority as King, God would reject. Many of the Jews then, and now, have in fact rejected Jesus and not accepted Him as their King and religious leader. So, according to God, Israel is no longer His chosen people."

John seemed sincerely interested. "I have never heard this before." He paused in thought. "If you are not Jews then you must be Catholic?"

Brad smiled again. "No. Not Catholic either. It was about 2,000 years ago when God's Son came to the earth. He began a new religion and a new church for all the people of the world. When that church began, believers called themselves, 'Christians.' They took the word 'Christian' after the one who gave His life for them. And from there, His one true church began. But a few hundred years later, many of the church leaders began to teach the opposite of what God had told them through the Bible. As a result, that group became known as the Catholic church.

John held Brad's gaze and said again, "I have never heard that either. The Catholic church is all over the world. Are not their leaders in Rome?"

"Just because they're big and there are many of them, does not make them right with God," Brad stated.

At that moment, Carol came over to the two men. She looked at John. "Mary is doing somewhat better. I'm hoping her fever will break soon." She took a deep breath. "John, I need to change the bandage and check your wound. Maybe this will be the last time I'll have to pack it."

"I am also hoping this will be the last time. That hurts a lot!" John said.

"I know, but it's doing its job by allowing the wound to heal from the inside out." Carol looked at Brad. "If you would, please move one of the chairs next to the window so I can get the most amount of light."

"I'd be glad to." Brad got up from his chair and slid it over to the window.

John turned to Brad as he sat down. "Can we talk again in a while?"

"Sure. I'm going to check on Kasey. I'll be back shortly."

Twenty minutes later Brad was back and Carol had finished wrapping John's wound. John sat down beside Mary,

who now sat upright on the couch. Mary spoke to John in Chinese, "Please ask Carol if you will get complete use of your arm when it is well?"

"The area around the wound is bruised so much that it's going to take a few weeks and some therapy to help it get back to normal," Carol stated matter-of-factly after John asked Mary's question.

Brad smiled and said, "John's keeping that arm in the sling so he won't be asked to help shovel snow!"

John smiled, held up his left arm and said, "I can help with this one!" They all chuckled.

Brad paused and pointed towards the driveway, "Kasey is out there and I think he is going to make it to the road tomorrow. He's got his sister helping him, and the further he gets from the house the snow is not as deep. Lord willing, maybe we'll get to your car tomorrow afternoon."

John said, "That will be good!"

Mary added, "It will be good to wear our own clothes again."

Brad moved the over-stuffed chair back to where it originally sat. Carol asked, "Can I get you two some hot coffee or tea?"

Both spoke at the same time. "Coffee."

"Great," said Carol. "I'll make a new pot and start lunch. How about potato soup with sausage in it?"

"That sounds good," Brad said.

Mary stood up with her blanket still wrapped around her. "I am going to go sit by the fire."

The two men settled in their chairs again. John turned to face Brad and said, "Around the world, there are Catholics and

Protestants who say they are Christians."

"You're right. A lot of people claim the name 'Christian.' But remember, people are not born into this world a Christian." He paused a second. "The term 'Christian' simply means a person who follows the teachings of Christ, the Son of God. They must become a Christian, one with Christ, then live life as a faithful Christian."

"What is a faithful Christian?" John asked, confused.

"My family and I are all faithful Christians. That means we have obeyed God's will for us, and we worship God in Spirit and truth as He requires. We are to put Him first in our hearts, our minds, and our souls. Also, we are to love our fellow man as we love ourselves. Of course, none of us are perfect. We do things on occasion that we should not, but we try to do our best. And when we fail to do that, God is willing to forgive us of our mistakes and disobedience to Him, providing we tell Him what we've done, and in our hearts we are truly sorry for what we've done, with the intention to never do it again."

John, hearing these things, sat puzzled. In his homeland and in his research, there were no people as Brad described. John asked, "Are the leaders of these true Christians only in America?"

"There are no leaders of these people on earth. The only leader is the Son of God, Jesus the Christ, who reigns over His people. His church is made up of these true Christians who serve Him."

John asked, "Are these true Christians only in America?"

Brad smiled. "No. Faithful Christians can be found in most every country in the world."

At that moment, Carol came through the door. "Lunch is ready."

The two men stood up and went toward the kitchen. John stopped in the living room and spoke in Chinese to Mary as she sat on the couch eating her soup.

CHAPTER 3

THE RESCUE

While the two men sat at the table in the kitchen enjoying their lunch, John asked Brad, "What do you do to make a living here in America?"

Brad took a spoonful of soup, swallowed, then answered, "I own a home construction company where we build houses in a manufacturing plant and then deliver them to the place where the home will be. We have three plants: one in Washington, one in Oregon, and one in Idaho. In these three places we produce four to ten houses per day, depending on the season of the year."

"I believe it is a good thing. Building homes for the people," John said.

"Carol said Mary told her that you do not live in America. You are here visiting?"

"Yes. We live in Beijing, China where I work for the government."

"So may I ask what you do for the government?"

"I am in charge of National Study and Control of the Population. Mary is my assistant."

"So, you are just here on vacation?"

"Yes," said John. "My boss thought it would be good for me to leave China for a few months because it looked like the

trouble on the border with Russia had gotten worse. But, we held them off and they are withdrawing because winter is now setting in along the border. We were heading home the day of the auto crash."

Brad, with a concerned frown, said, "John, do you believe there will be a war between your country and the Russians?"

"Yes, I am sure of it. Last summer the Russians had one army along our northern border. I think they were testing us. This summer, they had two armies at the border and our spies tell us they are preparing two additional armies to be moved to the front in the spring. I am certain they intend to overrun China. If they do, it will provide them a southern border to the Pacific Ocean. My government is in talks with America now for help in supplying us with tanks, guns, planes, and ships. They have made it clear they can sell us all we will need, but there is no way America will get involved in helping us with troops in China. America will not take part in another war, so we will be alone when it comes."

The front door opened and Kasey came in stomping snow off of his boots. "Dad! I made it to the road!"

"Great!" said Brad. "Did you see the car?"

"No, but I'm pretty sure I know where it is."

Brad got up, walked over to his son, gently slapped him on the back, and said, "Great job, Kasey. Go get something hot to drink and a shower. I know that will help you feel better. I think I'll go out and see the work you've done." Brad put on his coat and left.

Brad returned shortly, firmly closed the door, and turned toward those in the room. "Kasey did make it to the road and then some. And if it doesn't snow tonight, I think we can make it to the car tomorrow morning. If the sun stays out I'm pretty sure I can hike up the hill the next day."

"That's good news," Carol said as she helped Brad take

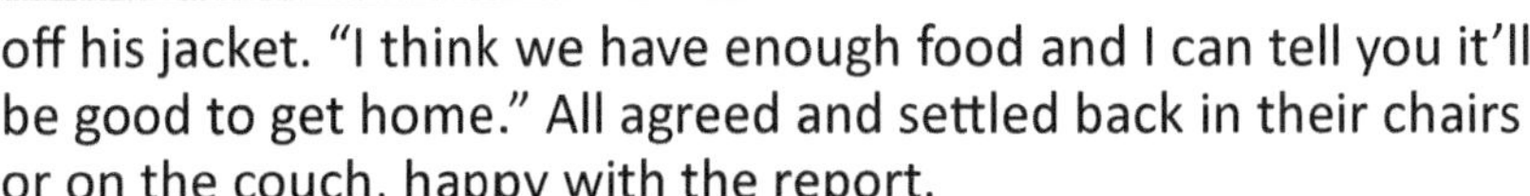

off his jacket. "I think we have enough food and I can tell you it'll be good to get home." All agreed and settled back in their chairs or on the couch, happy with the report.

Later that afternoon, Mary was asleep on the couch, Carol and Bailey were sitting near the fireplace reading books, and Kasey was in his room. Brad was back in his chair in front of the big window taking in the last rays of the afternoon sun, in one of those warm-sun cat naps.

John came out of his room to walk around in the house. He saw Brad in his chair and walked over and sat down next to him.

When John sat down, Brad woke up and straightened in his chair. "John, how are you feeling this afternoon?"

"I feel good. I do have a small headache. My shoulder is better but still tender."

"We've been praying that we will get you to the hospital in a couple of days so they will check it out. They probably need to x-ray it to know for certain nothing is broken."

John nodded and looked out the window as the sun was getting low in the sky. He gathered his thoughts and said to Brad, "I would like to ask you some more about these true Christians you were talking about this morning."

"Sure. What would you like to know?"

"Are these Christians all over the world?"

"Yes. I'm sure there are some in every nation."

John quickly responded, "There are none in China. I make it my job to know all there is to know about the people of China. As a population control official, I must know. It's my job to know these things."

Brad smiled and nodded. "Yes, they are there. You just haven't found them."

I could not have missed this kind of people, John thought to himself. "If you say they are all over the world, how many are there in America?"

Brad thought for a second. "No one knows for sure. Some estimate over one million in America and over two million worldwide. But as I said, no one knows. Only God knows for sure. Every day, God adds to His people."

"So, Brad, you are saying there may not be many percentage-wise in comparison to the world population of over seven billion people." John paused then asked, "If being a true Christian is that important, why are there so few?"

"First of all, there is an evil one who seeks to keep people from becoming one of these faithful Christians. Jesus Himself said the way one becomes a true Christian is not easy to find and the gate is not big at all, and only a few will choose to be a part. He also said that the other way is the direction most people will go. It's easy and the gate is wide. Most people will go through the wide gate, and they will not be with God."

"This does not make sense," John said. "Why didn't your God make it so most people would go where He is?"

"He could have, but He didn't. God does want all men to be with Him. But, most people choose not to. They want to live their lives free from His authority and obedience to Him. However, this separates them from God."

John looked at Brad, forming another question. "Do all these true Christians meet in some place in America or another country?"

"Well, no. There isn't a world meeting of true Christians. We are to meet with other faithful Christians who are living in our area every Sunday for the purpose of worshipping God and to honor His Son, Jesus, Who is our King and spiritual leader. And as a part of that gathering, it provides time for fellowship with each other."

At that moment, Kasey came over. "Dad, Mom said now that it's almost dark, you two could come over and join the rest of us in front of the fireplace and have some family time."

Brad looked over at John. "Shall we join them?"

John smiled. "Yes." Kasey and his dad moved the two big chairs.

At the fireplace, Carol had the coffee table covered with a tray of hot tea and hot chocolate, a dish of chocolate chip cookies that Bailey had made, and a bowl of popcorn. As they all sat around the fire, Kasey and Bailey sang a couple of songs, Carol read about spring and summer from her book of poetry, and Brad finished up with a reading from the Bible in James chapter one.

Brad finished, grinned at Kasey and said, "If you're going after the car first thing in the morning, you'd better get some rest. It's going to be a lot of hard work."

"Yes, sir," Kasey said with a big grin. He picked up his phone from a side table. "Got music for sleeping." He said goodnight to the others, but bent over and hugged his mother. "Mom, do you think you can spare three eggs and sausage for breakfast? I'll need all the energy I can get to make it to the car."

Carol laughed softly. "Sure, son. I think I have some eggs and sausage left."

"Thanks. See ya in the morning," he yelled back as he made the stairs two at a time.

"I think I should stay on the couch one more night," Mary said.

Carol and Bailey picked up the dishes.

"I'll say goodnight for Carol and I, and we'll see you in the morning." Brad excused himself from the room.

John and Mary replied, "Goodnight," to everyone, but

stayed up much longer talking in Chinese.

The next morning Kasey rose early to prepare the sled to take with them to the car. He pulled it around to the front of the house, stomped the snow off of his boots on the porch, then set them down. He walked to the fireplace in his socks, put more wood on the fire, and warmed himself a minute. He disappeared briefly, then returned with his ski poles where he leaned them against the wall beside his hiking boots. "Now I'm ready for the day's adventure," he said softly to himself. "Oh no, I'm not," he continued. He turned to Carol. "Hey, Mom, do I have time to go to the storage room before breakfast? I've got to find all the rope I can."

"Just don't take too long," Carol said.

Mary appeared at the kitchen door followed by Bailey. Carol greeted her daughter with a hug and smiled at Mary. Mary smiled back and said, "I heard you working. May I help?"

Carol studied Mary a moment. "You look much better today," she said. "Please, sit." She motioned to the table. She pointed to the stack of plates and utensils as she spoke to Bailey. "You can set the table." Bailey had barely finished when Brad, John, and Kasey came through the kitchen door and took their seats at the table.

Breakfast was eaten without conversation. The unspoken feeling for the adventure of finding the car and retrieving the luggage filled the air. It wasn't long before breakfast was done and everyone except Mary was bundled up to go with Kasey. Carol, Brad, and John agreed that Mary should stay in the house and keep warm.

It was cold but the sun was bright as everyone headed down the path. When a tree limb, heavy with snow, cracked loudly and fell, Brad watched it. "Kasey, stay in the road, away from the trees. The snow's weighing down those limbs and we don't know when they might fall."

A few minutes later Kasey paused and wound the rope

around one hand to get a better grip to pull the sled. He grabbed a snow shovel from the sled, then turned and headed off the road between some trees. "I think it's through here," he said. "But it may take a while to find."

"Just be careful, son," Brad said as Kasey headed through the trees.

It wasn't long before Kasey shouted, "I found the car!"

"Bailey and I are going back to the house to put on another pot of coffee and make hot chocolate for when you come in," Carol said. "You don't need us here anyway. We just needed to get out of the house."

Brad and John stood at the end of the snow-cleared path next to the road while Kasey shoveled snow to get into the car. Kasey tied four long ropes together then tied them to the sled so that his dad could pull the sled back when it was loaded.

While the two men waited at the end of the shoveled path, John asked, "Now these true Christians you spoke of, do they have an army? Do they in some way fight against other religions or people?"

Brad smiled and said, "Well, we are in the Lord's army and we do fight against evil in the world for the sake of others that we can help. Jesus has told us that we are to be at peace with all men as best we can and to do good to all people. In fact, He has taught us that we are to love our enemies and to do good to those who hate us. We are to even pray on behalf of our enemies and those who persecute us. We are to live like, and be like, our King and Savior, Jesus."

John looked confused at what Brad said. "I have never heard of a people exactly like that. For me, I do not believe I could do that."

"Yes, sometimes it's very hard," Brad agreed. "But we must do the best we can to live and think that way."

John stood in thought, trying to comprehend the

ramifications of what he had just been told. He asked again, "If these people have a king that you say rules over them, are they then against others who rule over them, like the government who rules over them now?"

"Well, as I've said before, the Son of God is our only King, religious leader, and Savior. But God has also told us that He has set up all earthly governments and authorities that exist in the world, and they are here for our good and the good of all people in every nation. Without governments and other authorities, there would be nothing but chaos in the world and maybe the evil one would rule over all of it. In America, our rulers are elected by the people. If we elect our leaders based upon God's principles, we get good, or better leaders. But if not, we get bad leaders. In your country, the leaders are there because of their power over the people much like most of the world is under the rule of kings or dictators. Either way, God expects not only true Christians, but all people, to have respect for and obedience to all governments and authorities who have rule over us no matter if they are good or bad government leaders. We are commanded to not even speak evil of any who have authority over us. There are no governments or authorities, good or bad, that exist in the world today that God has not allowed to exist. So as Christians, if we go against those who have authority over us, good or bad, then we are going against God's appointed rulers and we will have done wrong in God's eyes. As true Christians, if we do good in the eyes of the government, we should not fear them for God has placed them there for our own good. We must honor and respect them."

"In all my studies and research of people and populations, I have not found those who will show that kind of honor and respect for their government."

Brad continued, "There is something I must add to what I've said. There are some things that, if our government asks us to do or not to do we must disobey them, but even then, we must respect their authority."

John's interest peaked. "What kind of things?"

"Well, if the government said we could not meet on Sunday and worship, or told us to deny God or Jesus, that we could not do, even to the point of death. If the authority over us asked us to lie or in some way harm our neighbor, we could not do that. If the government required my wife or I to kill our unborn child, or take our own lives, these things we could not do, even if it meant our death."

John asked again, "Are these true Christians a cult? Do they live in communes?"

"No, they're not a cult and they live just like everyone else."

"Then how could I, or someone else, find them?"

"I've never been asked that question." Brad thought for a moment and said, "Well, we do meet together on each Sunday to worship God."

"Then is this Church a building some place?"

"The Church is the people of Christ, not a building or a place. The building could have a name on it like 'The Church of Jesus,' 'Christ's Church,' or 'The Church of Christ.' Either way, it will indicate who the owner is of the people who meet in that place. But even the name may not always indicate them, or His people who are worshipping God exactly how He has told them to do."

"Then all Christian churches are where these true Christians worship?"

"There are many good people who say they are Christians, but for whatever reason, do not worship God as He has commanded them to do. The true Christian who worships in the way God would have them to do is harder to find." Brad paused a moment before he went on to say, "Jesus said, 'Seek and you will find.' There will only be a few who find the Lord and worship Him in the way He has authorized. These true Christians are like salt that you would sprinkle on your food. The salt is not

easily seen, but you will taste it in your food. So is the Christian. He will be the salt of the earth."

Brad and John were still talking when Kasey yelled out, "I'm ready!" Brad picked up the rope and began to pull. John, wanting to help, did what he could with his left arm. Shortly, they saw the sled and Kasey pushing it. The trip back to the house didn't take as long, and soon the men brought in two large suitcases, two carry-ons, a laptop, and a briefcase.

John and Mary were happy to get their luggage back and stood smiling ear-to-ear. "We cannot thank you enough for your help," John said as he reached out to shake hands with Brad and Kasey. "Now excuse us, please. We want to go to our room, clean up, and change into our own clothes." Mary nodded quickly in agreement, already walking towards their room.

In the kitchen, Brad and Kasey warmed up with hot chocolate, and Kasey ate a second breakfast.

"Dad," Kasey said when he had taken his last bite. He motioned towards the other room when Brad looked at him. They both walked into the living room, but Kasey didn't stop until they had crossed over to the other side of the room. Kasey turned and said, "I didn't want Mom and Sis to hear what I'm going to say."

"What is it, son? You seem troubled."

"Dad, when I was getting the bags out of the car, one of the carry-ons had come open in the wreck and things were scattered on the floor and seat. When I went to put everything back in the bag, I couldn't help but notice that there were tens of thousands of dollars there, more money than I've ever seen." Kasey paused and stared at his dad a moment. "And that's not all. There was a gun in the bag with a loaded magazine in it. And the briefcase was open, and full of papers and everything was in Chinese."

"Son, they are Chinese, and people from other countries will sometimes use cash instead of a credit card. As far as the gun, well, with all that cash maybe he thinks he needs it."

"But Dad, they could be bank robbers or drug dealers even," Kasey argued, clearly agitated at the find. "And at best, maybe he's laundering money! Maybe they came down the old road to get away from the police."

Brad thought for a moment and let out a sigh. "Son, he told me that he worked for the Chinese government. Maybe that's why he has the cash. I don't think we should make too much of this."

"But Dad, I could be right! I don't think it would be safe to stay overnight with them. Anything could happen to us! And they could take our car and no one would've known they were here."

"Son, what are you trying to say?"

"When I was at the car, I took a good look at the snow on the road out of the canyon. On a clear day I've walked out of the canyon up that road in about an hour. I'm certain I can do it, even with the snow, in two hours. I'm sure!"

Brad looked at Kasey and considered his suggestion. "I would need to go with you in case there was any problem along the way."

"No Dad, you need to stay here in case there's any trouble. I can do this alone." Their gazes held as Kasey went on to say, "I'm going to be eighteen next week. I know I can do this. Trust me. And as soon as I get to the top of the canyon, the cell phone signals will be strong. They always have been. I can call 9-1-1 and we could be rescued and out of here in a few hours."

Brad looked long and hard at his son as he thought about what to do. "Okay, son. Put some dry clothes on and rest for at least an hour. I'll talk with your mother and tell the others what's going on."

A little over an hour later, Brad and Kasey were at the end of the path next to the road going out of the canyon.

"Son, do you have everything you need?"

"Yes, sir. I have three bottles of water and all of our cell phones. Mom made me two sandwiches. I'm okay here."

Brad discreetly handed Kasey a gun and said, "This is your mother's pistol. When you get halfway up the hill, I want you to fire one round so I know where you are. And when you reach the top and have been able to contact 9-1-1, be sure and tell them that we need snow plows and gravel trucks. Then fire two shots so I know that you made it."

"And we need the police for our guests," Kasey added.

"Now son," Brad said softly. "Don't say anything except there's been a car accident, someone's been hurt, and the police need to come and check it out."

"Okay Dad, but while I'm gone, you need to be really careful."

"And you, too, son. Don't go near the trees. Big limbs can break from the weight of the heavy snow."

"Yes, sir. I'll stay in the middle of the road."

Brad hugged his son and sent him off. As Kasey made his way down the road and up the hill, Brad watched for as long as he could see him. Then he stopped and prayed. "Father, please keep all of us safe, but especially Kasey."

Only fifty minutes had passed when Brad heard the single shot to let him know Kasey was half way. It was cold and Brad gladly went back into the house to tell the others that Kasey had made it past the halfway mark.

With pent-up nervous energy, Brad paced around and around the living room while keeping an eye on the clock. He lost track of the times around the room, and how often he had checked the time. When he looked again, only three minutes had passed. *Time is crawling,* he thought to himself. *I'm going back outside after another thirty minutes and wait for the next signal.*

Carol and Bailey sat by the fireplace talking about things they needed to do when they got home. John and Mary conversed in Chinese as they sat by themselves in the two chairs in front of the big window.

Brad couldn't wait. He went outside to the path, even though it was still twenty minutes before the expected time of the second signal. Two hours came and went. Nothing. Ten more minutes passed. Twenty minutes. No signal. Brad prayed again, "Father, I'm asking You to keep my son safe."

At two hours and thirty minutes Brad began to wonder what had happened and said into the air, "I think I need to go up the hill and check." It was impossible to see very far up the road because of the sun's glare reflecting off the snow. "Okay," Brad continued the conversation with himself. "I need to go back into the house and prepare to hike the canyon myself." At that moment he heard two single shots come from the top of the canyon. Brad sighed in relief and prayed again, "Thank You, Lord for keeping Kasey safe, and for our safety as well."

Brad headed back to the house. As he came through the front door he yelled, "Start packing. Get ready to close down the house! We'll be out of here in three or four hours!"

Less than two hours later everyone had packed and was ready to close up the house. Brad put all of the family's luggage in their SUV and took another minute to walk out and look up the road to see what he might see at the top of the canyon. Blinking emergency lights from different vehicles turned slowly downward. Brad felt they would reach the house within a couple of hours.

When Brad went back into the house to tell the others about help arriving, he saw that John and Mary had put all of their luggage in one place. He saw the two carry-on bags and remembered about the money and the gun. *If the police came about the accident and the two indeed are wanted, they will deal with it. I don't need to worry about it.*

A few minutes later, Brad stood at the large bay window, looking at the snow glistening on the canyon floor in the afternoon sun. As he did so, he offered a short prayer, "Thank You, Father, for the upcoming rescue, and bringing us safely to this time."

John walked up beside him and also looked out the window. "Brad, you think they will be here soon?"

"I think so. Maybe an hour or an hour and a half."

"In my country in all of the schools, we are taught that there is no God and that the world came into existence by chance and evolution over millions of years, and that is what I believe today. We are also taught that religion is for the weak that need to believe in something. The government allows only Buddhists, Catholics, some Protestants, Muslims, and Hindus to exist as religious groups, and they do that for the sake of the weak and the poor. But most people in my great country, like me, believe there is no God."

Brad thought a second or two and then said, "Believing is based upon fact that proves there is a God."

"So you're telling me there is proof for the existence of a God?"

"Wait here. I'll be right back." In less than five minutes Brad returned. Mary was there talking to John in Chinese.

Brad stood patiently until Mary left. He held a Bible out to John. "This is mine. I want you to have it. All of the things we have talked about are in there, and the answers to all of your questions are there, too. If you will look into it and study it, you will find that belief in God is not based upon feeling but upon evidence and truth only. You will know for sure that, in fact, it was by the power and authority of the will of God that the earth and all that is in it was made for His Son, and that all that was made was done so through the power and authority of Jesus Christ. You will also learn that when the time was right, God gave His Son to be a sacrifice for the sins of all mankind. And, that Jesus was willing to give up what He had in heaven with His Father, come to the earth, and freely give His life on behalf of all of us. Then God His Father brought Him back to life and gave Jesus, His Son, all authority over all people while we are here on earth, and also when we go to heaven."

Brad took a breath. "This book will also tell you that His Son, Jesus, will come back some day and take with Him to heaven those special children of God, those true Christians who have followed all of what Jesus told them to do. And there in heaven they will all live in great pleasure for everlasting." Brad paused, then finished, "And John, I also placed a note in the book for you so that you can know how to identify these special people of God."

NOTE:

How you can identify one of God's people

- *They are ones who believe God and know that Jesus the Christ is His Son, the Savior of all mankind.*

- *They are the ones who have confessed to God and Christ their sins, or wrong doing, and promised the Lord not to ever do those things again. They repented of their sins.*

- *They are people who are willing, no matter what, to declare to anyone the fact that Jesus Christ is the Son of the living God, and that He is Lord and Savior of the world.*

- *They are also the ones who have been baptized in the way God has instructed in His Word. They have done this for the remission of their past sins before God.*

- *After becoming one of these special people of God, a Christian, they will do their very best every day to live and worship God as He has instructed them to do in this book, the Bible. They will also, all the days of their life, place God and His Son first in their life above any and all else, even unto death.*

By this time, the snow plows could be heard outside the house. Everyone rushed out to see. The plows were followed by the gravel trucks spreading gravel, a red emergency vehicle, and a state police car.

The rescuers wasted no time getting in the house. The EMTs began to check John's wound and possible bone breakage in his shoulder. Carol told them what she had done for the wound. The policeman talked to John about his side of the story of the accident. Brad stood nearby to hear what the policeman had to say as John explained what had happened.

The police asked John for his driver's license. Seeing that it was an international license, he asked, "Are you U.S. citizens?"

"No."

The policeman asked for their passports. Looking over the passports, he said, "You two are wanted people."

Kasey was right after all, Brad thought.

The policeman said to John, "You are on my Missing Persons list, reported by the Chinese Consulate in San Francisco. They will be happy to know that you are okay. You will need to contact them as soon as you get to town."

One of the EMTs said, "We're ready to go and will transport these two people to the Tahoe hospital to get them checked out."

"Good," the policeman said, and added, "If everyone's leaving, I'll work on my report and follow all of you out of the canyon in case there's any other problem."

Kasey and Bailey carried the couple's luggage to the emergency vehicle. John and Mary again thanked Brad and Carol for all they had done for them. With hugs and handshakes, they said their goodbyes and soon they were all in their vehicles and on their way out of the canyon, leaving the snowy nightmare behind.

CHAPTER 4

THE EAGLE NEWS

A little over two years later, in mid-March, Brad and Carol celebrated their twenty-fifth wedding anniversary. Bailey was a senior, homeschooled by her mother, expecting to graduate in June. She was trying to decide whether to go to college or to start working in the family home-building business. Kasey was in college at Oregon State where he played basketball. Brad's business had been very slow during the winter months but had begun to pick up for the coming summer, as it usually did.

American politics was like always with nothing getting done. Political correctness had its grip on the country, quickly running it down.

America was the most in-debt country in the world, with the debt amount beyond what anyone could have imagined.

The military had been reduced to smaller than before World War II.

Hundreds of thousands of people had continued to pour into the U.S. along the southern borders, but now they came from every country in the world.

America seemed morally, politically, and religiously bankrupt. America's leadership had lost respect among most countries of the world.

In the rest of the world, there continued to be small wars and rumors of wars, and America was determined not to get involved in any of it.

For the last three years, during the spring and summer months, there had been a fierce border war between Russia and China along the Chinese northern border. Each year it seemed to become harder to stop clashes between the armies, and reports of casualties were growing. These two great armies seemed to be determined to mount a full-scale war.

The Russians had built two large armies near Moscow, and now had the largest military in the world. To encounter the threat from the Russians, China was building the second largest army. As the richest nation, China had the money to secure all of the latest and greatest military hardware for their defense. They knew if the Russians took over, they would gain all of China's wealth. The Russians then would have a thousand miles of southern coastline in the Pacific Ocean and from there, Japan, South Korea, and all of Asia could be theirs for the taking.

For the past two years, China had begged America many times to send their military to come and help them. The American people and the government were against getting into any war anywhere.

China, Japan, and South Korea were America's biggest trading partners, and supplied America with over two-thirds of all her manufacturing needs and goods. America had no choice but to give China everything they had to help them stop the Russians.

China also had much of America's debt, and all the money she seemed to need. She was buying weapons from anywhere she could. Even throughout America she was buying civilian rifles to supply her ever-growing army.

As the new year began, America had a new government, elected the previous November. The people had elected a new party that had run on the promises of keeping America out of the looming Russian-Chinese war in eastern Europe. Even the former government had not wanted to see America involved in another war, but because China was her largest trading partner, the new government knew that China had to be given everything she needed to protect herself, not only on her northern borders, but from a certain naval attack along her southern borders of the Pacific. The Russians had also built the largest Navy in the world.

America was helping supply every new and surplus military weapon available, even though China also received an endless supply of equipment and arms from England and other countries. America had sent 6,000 top U.S. military personnel to train the Chinese military with the latest American equipment and tactics. She also supplied most all of America's latest planes and training to what was becoming the largest Air Force. The whole world knew that war had been building up for three years now and all of the experts believed that it would begin in the coming spring.

China trembled at the prospects of what was about to happen. The Russians had bought up much of the world's supply of steel as they raced to build their Navy, and were now on the verge of bankruptcy, having spent all they had and more on men and arms. The experts knew that if Russia failed at their attempt to take China, they would collapse financially and never recover. She could not dare lose because she had everything to gain: the wealth of the richest nation in the world, and a billion people she could control for her own wants and desires. Everyone knew there were going to be desperate times ahead.

For the previous two winters, Russia had moved almost all of her Navy from their frozen ports and harbors along their northern coast in the Arctic Ocean, south to winter in ports throughout the Mediterranean, and their larger ships in ports from Spain, Portugal, and southward to Morocco. Each year those ports were so congested with ships that surrounding countries complained to the U.N. But on the other hand, those countries were glad because of the money the Russian Navy spent with them over the months of November through February.

This year, some of the largest ships appeared to be

practicing military maneuvers, often passing back and forth through the Suez Canal from the Mediterranean into the Red Sea. But there was one thing missing. For almost ten years Russia had been secretly building an all-new type of submarine fleet. Not much was known about them except that they were large and many of them carried missiles. It was also thought that some of the largest ones carried troops.

American military experts who studied the Russians always wanted to know where the subs were. Reports had been received for years from fishermen saying they had seen subs at night off the coast of Greenland. Over the last two years, most reports came from the South China Sea off the coast of Vietnam, and as far north as the Sea of Japan. Even in North America there had been a couple of sightings in the Hudson Bay, and some along the coast of Brazil. Most experts believed they were hidden in the North Pacific along the Russian border to be ready for the naval invasion of South China.

Most all of the Russian Air Force was now carrier based, with six large carriers and up to ten smaller ones. There were three armies just to the north of China, and Kazakhstan and Mongolia both knew the Russians would easily cross their borders and take them over as they moved into China.

Reports spread from the intelligence community that North Korea was planning to attack South Korea when the war started, and that Iran was planning to attack Iraq, Saudi Arabia, and Kuwait at the same time to gain control of all the eastern oil. Muslims throughout North Africa and Western Europe were also planning to take over all the governments they could while the Russian-Chinese war distracted the world. The whole world was poised for the greatest war in Europe since World War II ended in 1945.

Brad Wilson arrived for work at 7:30 a.m. West Coast time to get ready for another day. At 8:32 a.m. one of the ladies ran to his office door and shouted, "Mr. Wilson! Come quickly! We're under attack!"

When Brad entered the lunchroom, everyone else was already there looking at the large-screen TV. As Brad stood off to the side, the reporter said, "The United States is under attack along the East Coast. Hundreds of fast, low-flying missiles have hit military bases as far west as Illinois. The missiles came in along the East Coast from Maine to Florida. Reports are coming in that Gulf Coast military bases were hit in Texas and others as far north as Kansas."

The lunchroom group sat frozen in stunned silence, all eyes glued to the television screen.

The news screen suddenly switched to a different studio at Eagle News. Bill Sawyer, a co-anchor, appeared on-screen surrounded by large monitors. He stood thoughtfully, head slightly bowed as he waited to begin what would be the most historical report of his life.

When the signal came, he straightened, took a deep breath and said, "Ladies and gentlemen, the United States of America came under attack at 11 a.m. Eastern Standard Time today." He paused. "From Maine to Florida. From Florida to Texas..." He turned to the big wall screen on his right. "Video reports taken by individuals and news organizations are coming in from around the country."

One by one video clips filled the screen showing people looking toward the Atlantic Ocean and the Gulf of Mexico. Sawyer continued. "Ladies and gentlemen, watch closely. Pretend you're standing on the coastline. Every two or three minutes you will see a missile launch just off the horizon. Try to focus on the rocket-like weapon as it passes overhead. Notice how fast they travel and how low they fly, parallel to the ground, much like a cruise missile." He turned from the monitor to face the camera. "There are literally thousands of reports coming into our office here at Eagle News."

He walked over to another wall-sized monitor and said, "We are going live to David Wade, our reporter assigned to Washington, D.C." As he spoke, the camera focused on the young blond reporter standing on the balcony of a building.

Sawyer said, "David, tell us what you know from there in D.C."

David rushed to get his microphone hooked up to make his report. When he began to speak, his voice quivered. "After seeing your report, we understand how widespread this attack is." He took a quick breath. "What I am now going to show you is truly unbelievable." The camera slowly panned off the reporter to the right. In the camera's view were the remains of what once was the Pentagon, nothing now but a hexagon-shaped pile of rubble on the ground.

Brad, watching everything on the screen, felt his blood run cold.

The young reporter's voice cracked as he continued, "The headquarters of the United States military stood here for many years. It's like a huge bomb blew it apart from the inside out, and yet, it's more than that. It looks like it disintegrated, like nothing we've ever seen before. The pile of rubble is small." The camera continued to scan the area where the Pentagon building once stood, fire and smoke rising from the rubble, numerous emergency vehicles with their flashing lights, and hundreds of people scurrying around trying to see what they might do to help. Sirens could be heard in all parts of the city.

David went on, "Eye witnesses said that one of the missiles crossed over the city of Washington and turned down into the open area, right in the middle of the Pentagon building. There was a high-pitched whine followed by what sounded like a string of firecrackers going off. Then there was a sound like a bomb going off, and the building seemed to disintegrate from the inside out. In less than a minute, nothing was left but piles of rubble. Not a wall was left standing."

Back in Oregon, comments poured forth throughout the lunchroom.

"How could this have happened?"

"God help us! We are at war."

"This can't be! Not here!"

A couple of the ladies sat and cried quietly. A few of the men vowed revenge. Brad stood in shock, speechless.

One of the employees asked Brad. "What should we do?"

Brad mentally shook himself out of his shock and answered firmly, "I believe we should go to our families and homes, and pray as much as we can for our nation and our military."

Most shook their heads and accepted that as the plan. But one young man had a different idea. "Not me. I'm heading east to join up to fight the invaders."

As everyone turned to leave the room, Brad looked back at the TV. The young reporter said, "We have not seen anything like this since the collapse of the Trade Center Towers in New York on 9/11."

Brad mumbled to himself as he grabbed a chair facing the center of the television screen and sat down. "I don't want to watch this, but I have to know what's going on for the sake of my family."

The screen transitioned back to Eagle Studios in New York where Bill Sawyer came on again. "We have just learned that all commercial planes have been ordered to land immediately, and to stay down to keep the air clear for military aircraft. All planes outside the U.S. have been told to turn back and not to enter U.S. airspace. We are also receiving reports that nearly every Naval fighting vessel from New York to Newark has been sunk or destroyed. We understand that there were two large carriers stationed on the East Coast. Both were hit at the docks and are now burning. Two other large carriers are stationed on the West Coast, and all of our other carriers have been loaned to the Chinese." Sawyer paused then said, "We are now going to Studio B."

With a short graphic that said, "BREAKING NEWS," the

network switched to Frank Summers, Eagle TV News Anchor. He looked straight into the camera and began. "We now believe this sneak attack on our nation has come from a large number of Russian submarines off our East Coast. Since 11 a.m. Eastern Standard Time, it is estimated that over 4,000 missile-type weapons have hit every Army, Navy, Marine, and Air Force base as far west as Texas and north to Ohio. So far, the only cities reported hit by these missiles were those with military bases."

Summers paused and turned to look at a small monitor on his desk, then continued. "We are told the attacks were so devastating that the Air Force has only a few planes not damaged, and they went east to attack the submarines that had surfaced off the coast."

Summers faced the camera again. "It is now 1 o'clock here in New York. We have also received reports that a number of our satellites are not working, and those that are, are not working well. The internet is down in several areas, and many are without cell phone service."

Summers paused again to look at the small monitor in front of him. He frowned. His forehead wrinkled. He raised his head and his eyes met the camera straight-on. "Ladies and gentlemen, we are receiving reports from countries around the Mediterranean that all of the Russian ships that appeared to be headed east have now turned, heading westward into the Atlantic with six large aircraft carriers leading the way. We must believe they are headed to the United States. Experts are telling us those carriers can be off our east coast in four to six days, and their aircraft can reach us in three days or less. All other troops and support ships, perhaps as many as four hundred total, can make the crossing in seven to nine days."

In New York City, near Times Square, two black SUVs pulled up outside the Eagle News headquarters. Three men got out of each vehicle. An older clean-shaven, well-dressed man stepped from the front passenger side of the first car, as another casually-dressed man with a graying, neatly-trimmed beard stepped out of the front passenger side of the second car. The other four men wore dark clothing and dark sunglasses, and each carried an AK 74 Russian assault weapon. No one smiled as they entered the Eagle News building.

A security guard said as they came through the door, "Good afternoon, Mr. Blackburn." Mr. Blackburn passed the guard, but did not acknowledge the greeting. Without a pause, he headed straight to the bank of elevators. All of the men but one entered the elevator. The remaining man stood quietly in the lobby, armed and watching for trouble.

The men exited the elevator on the eighth floor and headed in the direction of the meeting room. A number of employees stopped working to observe the procession. Another one of the armed men remained near the elevator.

Mr. Blackburn passed by a desk where an older, well-dressed woman sat. "I want Mr. Foster, all of the producers, directors, and any news people in this building up here right now. NOW!"

"Yes sir!" she replied quickly as she picked up the phone.

Mr. Blackburn and the other man walked straight into the conference room, followed by the two remaining armed men.

In Studio C, Shirley Steele was just going on the air. "It's hard to know where to start exactly. America has been under attack since 11 a.m. this morning. We here at Eagle are literally receiving thousands of reports every hour. There are so many we cannot confirm them. Cell phones and internet are down in many areas around the U.S., but we can see from video footage that right now only the military has received the brunt of the attack."

Screens began showing videos, one after another, of military bases and air fields completely destroyed. Shirley continued, "Reports are coming from as far west as Kansas City, all along the Gulf Coast states across Texas, and into Oklahoma. Some reports indicate that it appears to be near total destruction with extremely high casualties among all of our military bases over half of the U.S. There are no reports of any large cities being hit by missiles."

Shirley stopped suddenly and put a hand to her ear, waited, then spoke again. "We are going back to David Wade in Washington, D.C."

The camera focused on the young reporter standing on the steps of the Federal Capitol Building. Shirley asked, "David, what's going on there?"

"Shirley, the city is quickly becoming a ghost town," he replied in a somber tone. "I'm told that every highway and road out of the city is clogged with cars, even thousands of people walking along the roads. Everyone believes an attack on the city is coming soon." Wade looked around quickly then continued. "I can tell you this. There are a few determined military, police, and government people who are doing all they can to secure national treasures and government buildings, and have taken it upon themselves to stay in these buildings, and protect our national archives at all cost. We have already heard of looting and robbing of food stores, gas stations, and drug stores in the downtown area of the city."

Two men suddenly appeared behind David, distracting him. He turned his back on the camera a moment, then faced the camera again and said, "We have with us now General Walter Parker, retired."

The General stepped up beside David. "General Parker, thank you for coming here to help the American people understand what has happened."

The General paused a moment to get his composure. "David, the American military was hit by a surprise attack today. I'm afraid it's so devastating that we do not have any reliable military force this side of the Rocky Mountains. What we do know is that all of our military has been ordered to re-form in places west of Sioux Falls, Omaha, and Topeka, where no rockets have hit. We believe that's out of their range."

The young reporter pointed toward where the Pentagon had stood and asked, "General, how bad is it really since we have now lost the Pentagon?"

The General looked in the direction of the Pentagon where smoke still rose from fires in the rubble. After a moment, he turned back to the camera and said, "Son, it took out almost all of our military command and communication support." He turned and took a second look in that direction, then turned back. He hesitated a moment longer, then said, "It's worse than that. Today at 10:30 there was a meeting in the Pentagon with all of our military leaders and the best of our military strategists from West Point, the U.S. Air Force Academy, and the Naval Academy. They were meeting with military leaders and government people from China to evaluate and consider what they believed was the upcoming war between China and Russia." The General turned and looked at the reporter and said, "Son, the best military minds we had were in there today. The enemy must have known that. I have to go now. Many of us veterans will be taking trains tonight, going west to do what we can to help organize what is left of the military."

Blessed be the name of God forever and ever, for wisdom and might are His. And He changes the times and the seasons; He removes kings and raises up kings; He gives wisdom to the wise and knowledge to those who have understanding.
-Daniel 2:20-21

Do not curse the king, even in your thought; Do not curse the rich, even in your bedroom. -Ecclesiastes 10:20

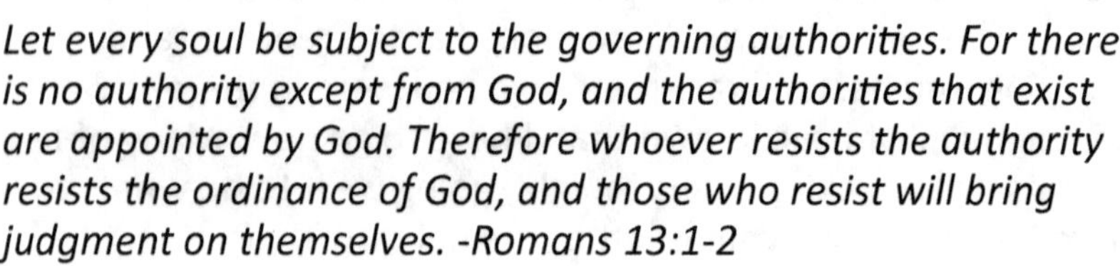

Let every soul be subject to the governing authorities. For there is no authority except from God, and the authorities that exist are appointed by God. Therefore whoever resists the authority resists the ordinance of God, and those who resist will bring judgment on themselves. -Romans 13:1-2

CHAPTER 5

THE RUSSIAN

In the conference room on the 8th floor, about thirty men and women were there at the demand of Mr. Blackburn, owner of Eagle News. An unknown, gray-bearded man, accompanied by two armed men, stood to his left. The employees whispered among themselves as to what might be going on. Someone asked, "Are these government men?"

Roger Foster, Manager of Eagle News, arrived last and stood near the front of the room. When all were assembled, Mr. Blackburn brought the group to order and gestured toward the other man on his left. "This is Zachar Polasky. He is an agent of the Russian Government. He has brought me here, but not of my own free will. He wanted to speak to me alone, but when I understood the situation, I told him I would not talk to him further, that he would have to speak with all of you."

Mr. Blackburn gestured to the Russian to go ahead, took a step back, crossed his arms, and waited to hear what the Russian agent had to say. Zachar looked slowly across the group and said, "I am only one of the many agents of my government who are in the process of taking over your government and nation."

Every person in the room spoke up vigorously at once against what had just been said. The two armed men immediately raised their guns, pointing them towards the group and chambering their first rounds. Everyone suddenly became quiet, not moving, realizing the men could and would kill them if signaled to do so.

Zachar continued, "I'm here to offer Eagle News a deal of a lifetime."

Roger Foster and two others from the audience spoke up at the same time. "We don't make deals with our enemy."

Zachar raised his hands, palms out, and said, "Okay. No deal. Your loss."

Another voice from the group said, "We don't deal."

Another said, "You'll never take this country."

Zachar turned to walk away but Mr. Blackburn spoke up, "Wait."

Zachar stopped and turned to face Mr. Blackburn and the group. Mr. Blackburn looked at the group and said, "I'm not agreeing to any deal, but I think we need to hear him out. It may be important and we are still in the news business." The group settled a bit, some shaking their heads. They all looked distrustfully at the Russian.

Mr. Blackburn turned back to Zachar and said, "Go ahead. We will hear you out."

Zachar began again. His voice and demeanor exuded confidence and authority. "The new government intends for there to be only one news broadcasting company in this country to provide news about all military and government activity. I have made the decision that it will be Eagle News. If that is not possible, I have a second and third choice."

One of the producers asked, "What about all of the other networks and local radio and television stations? Do you think they will do nothing?"

Zachar replied, "They will be able to continue broad-casting anything, including local news and weather, but all national news they will take as a feed from Eagle News."

A man in the group spoke up, "And what makes you think

they're going to go along with that?"

"Oh, they will be glad to take your feed because if they do not, they will experience some very bad things going wrong with their transmitters, towers, and cable systems. And if that is not enough, the owners and management will find themselves in Russia helping out the war effort in a work camp. Do I make the picture clear?"

Another man asked "Are you saying that is what will happen to us if we say no?"

Zachar spoke only one word with calm finality. "Precisely."

Mr. Foster asked, "Why did you choose Eagle News?"

Zachar said, "I have studied all of the broadcasting networks and especially Eagle. Communicating with the people is very important at a time like this. They need to know the news and they must trust the news they get or they will not believe it. I believe that Eagle does the best job at giving the people what you call 'true and reliable news.' It's important for the viewers to get that now."

A lady from the group spoke. "So you are going to tell us what we can and cannot say to make this true and reliable Russian news?"

Zachar smiled slightly then replied, "No, not at all. You are free to provide the news, true and reliable, for all the people. They will need your help."

"So we could embed our reporters within your military so that you would be able to take over the news?"

"If we do this, many people will see us as spies working for your people."

"This place could be overrun and we could all be killed by our own people."

"Yes! What about that?"

Zachar barely smiled as he thought to himself, *They are beginning to understand their predicament.* Then he said to the group, "That is true, but as fair news broadcasters, people will begin to trust you for providing them important information and realize you had no other choice." Zachar paused. "It will also be the responsibility of the state and city governments to protect you and Eagle News at all cost."

One of the men from the group sarcastically asked, "What makes you think they're going to do that?"

"Oh, I know they will," Zachar answered confidently as he pulled a red cell phone out of his pocket. Looking down at it, he said, "You must decide now what you are willing to do." He raised the phone for the group to see and said, "You only have about 24 minutes to decide."

Mr. Blackburn asked, "Can you give us time to talk among ourselves?"

Zachar replied, "You have 23 minutes left, and I am not leaving this room."

The group and Mr. Blackburn moved to the other side of the room, turned their backs to the Russian agent, and began to speak in low-whispered tones among themselves.

Zachar sat down in a nearby chair holding the red phone. The two armed men stood beside him like attack dogs waiting for a command.

Three minutes went by and a man among the group turned, visibly upset, and left the room. Five minutes later a woman left the room crying. After twelve minutes the group turned back around. Mr. Blackburn walked toward Zachar and the Russian rose.

Mr. Blackburn said, "My company and its employees who are here now believe we should continue to broadcast the news for the sake of the American people. As long as we have the right to tell the whole truth, and we are not forced to become a propaganda machine for you or anyone else." He stopped briefly, then continued, "Now, how can we know that the employees and our families will be safe when the war gets worse? And if any employee does not want to stay, are they free to go?"

Zachar looked at Mr. Blackburn, then at the group of men and women, "Is that all?"

"It is for now," Mr. Blackburn replied.

Zachar shook his head slightly and said, "You shall continue to own and operate this business as you have, and any employee is free to come or go as your management determines." He stopped and made eye contact with a few in the group before going on. "As for your safety, I cannot guarantee it because the world is full of crazy people. But this building will be completely emptied of anyone who is not an Eagle News employee. There will be security 24-hours-a-day like these," he said as he gestured to the two armed men beside him. "All doors will be locked and barricaded at all times. Only employees and family may enter. You are free to move all employees' families either into this building or a nearby hotel. I believe the City Police and the National Guard will also provide security for all of you."

A man from the group asked, "Again, what makes you think they're going to do that?"

Zachar smiled. "Oh, they will do that." He went on to say, "All employees will have a special security pass and reporters who travel outside the city will be given a special travel pass that will be accepted by the new government and its army anywhere they go. I personally will move into this building with my staff of news reviewers. I will be with you from now on. As far as broadcasting the news true and reliable, you can. Just remember, no secrets, codes, or messages in your news. No disrespect to the old government or the new government. If you deal only with the facts and you make certain those facts are true, you will do well. If any employee is caught doing anything secretive or underhanded, you have my word they will

immediately be removed from the building and shot. If I believe the whole management is involved, then I, and my people, will leave and this building and all who are in it will be like your Pentagon is today. For your safety you must put in place people who will make sure that all stories you broadcast are checked for truth and accuracy. Your lives will depend upon it." All faces in the group soberly reflected understanding.

Isidro Morales, an Eagle News Correspondent, middle-aged with a graying mustache spoke up, "Mr. Blackburn, if it's okay, I would like to volunteer to be embedded in the enemy's army."

Mr. Blackburn stared at the man a moment. "Isidro, are you sure you are willing to risk your life?"

"Yes sir, I do. It's a once-in-a-lifetime opportunity to let the people know what's going on."

Mr. Blackburn gestured towards Zachar. "It's up to him."

Zachar looked at Isidro and said, "Can you be ready in three days?"

Isidro answered without hesitation, "Yes sir, I can."

Zachar raised the hand with the red phone and began to key in his message. In a few seconds he received some kind of answer and turned to those in the room. "You are now the National News Broadcasting Company, NNBC." Zachar turned to Mr. Blackburn. "Who has the news broadcast at 8 p.m.?"

"Wayne Cannon, but he's not here yet."

"As soon as he is here and you have met with him, and if he chooses to still work for you, then I want a meeting with the two of you, his producers, and all of his staff."

"I'll see what I can do," said Mr. Blackburn.

Within a half hour, everything happened as Zachar had said. Reports came in from all of the national broadcasters acknowledging that all national news they would be broadcasting from that time on would come through the National News Broadcasting Company. And within two hours there was a large increase of security agents with their Russian assault rifles, standing at every door and other strategic places around the building.

Connie Cooper, Journalist and Political Commentator, was on the air from Studio C. "This day has been a national tragedy. Every military base in the eastern half of the United States has been destroyed or is certainly unusable." She paused. "Some reports estimated that loss of life could be from 50,000 to 250,000 military personnel and civilian base workers. We know that all military personnel have been ordered to be re-formed into military defensive units west of Kansas City. These forces and others in the west are what is left to defend against the invasion." Connie paused again briefly. "We are now going to Gene Hocker, chairman of the FAA."

Mr. Hocker's somber, middle-aged face appeared on the screen. "Mr. Hocker, can you tell us what you know about the airlines and air travel?"

"Yes, Connie," he responded. "All airlines are grounded and are expected to stay grounded. There are a few military aircraft in the air and some private aircraft, most all going west, with a few going north and south out of the country. Emergency helicopters and some news copters are working on our military bases to help the wounded. No aircraft is leaving from the East Coast, nor are there any planes approaching the East Coast. There are still some planes, commercial and private, coming and going west of the Rocky Mountains, in California, Oregon, and Washington. And . . ."

"Thank you Mr. Hocker," Connie interrupted. "We are now going back to David Wade in Washington, D.C." The incoming signal from David was fuzzy but clear enough to see. "Can you tell us what's happening from the nation's capital?"

"Connie, the city is a ghost town," David said as the camera man scanned the empty streets, the Capitol building,

and the White House. "We are on top of the Lincoln Memorial." He paused to look at his notes, then continued, "We understand that the White House has been evacuated. The president and his advisors, the Supreme Court, and both houses of Congress have been taken to a secret location outside the city. Tonight we understand that they will be moved someplace where the government can operate more securely."

The camera stopped panning and focused on the rubble where the Pentagon had been. David stood silent and reverent, allowing viewers time to take in the horrible scene. Then he ended his report. "Connie, tonight we ask all Americans to pray for our nation in its time of peril. To pray especially for our military and others who were lost today in this sneak attack upon our country. Pray for the families of those who were lost. And pray for all of our leaders at this tragic time in our nation."

Zachar sat in one of the guest chairs where he could see over the entire Eagle News' main control room with his armed agents behind him. The room held over one-hundred monitors of various sizes, showing news feeds from around the world. Men and women were positioned to control the video footage coming in from the six studios located within the Eagle News building. Twenty to thirty people were in the room at various times during any given 24 hours, all with different jobs that worked together to be able to broadcast the news stream continuously without a glitch or delay.

One of the Eagle's female producers came to Zachar. "Mr. Blackburn and Mr. Cannon are available in room B," she said.

Zachar, the producer, and one of the agents entered the room. The other agent closed the door and stood outside.

Mr. Blackburn, Wayne Cannon, two producers, and four other staff employees were there, talking among themselves. When Zachar entered, they stopped talking and sat back in their chairs. An empty chair sat at the end of the long conference table, and to the right of it sat Mr. Blackburn. Across from him, to the left of the empty chair sat Mr. Cannon and his staff.

The Russian agent walked up and put his hands on the back of the empty chair. "This is Zachar Polasky," Mr. Blackburn said to those at the table, then he introduced Cannon and the others to the Russian. The atmosphere was one of strained politeness.

Mr. Blackburn spoke directly to Zachar. "I have told this group everything that was said in our meeting earlier, and that you requested a meeting with them."

Cannon spoke up in a stern but agitated voice as the two men looked eye to eye. "I want to ask you a question first."

"Ask your question," Zachar directed with a smirk, as if he knew what Cannon was going to say.

Still stern and on the verge of anger, Cannon said, "What if one of us has an automatic weapon under this table, we pull it out and kill you and your gunman there? We would have the first two dead Russians of the war."

Zachar looked at Cannon for a few seconds. "I'm sure that thought has crossed your mind."

"Yes, it has," Cannon confessed without hesitation.

Zachar's voice grew stern. "I think you could do that, but I don't believe you want the consequences of your actions. Within minutes all of your fellow employees in this building, their families, and maybe as many as a million of your New York City neighbors would pay a dear price for your actions." He paused then added, "Mr. Cannon, I believe you and your fellow employees should do all you can to make sure nothing happens to me."

At that point Cannon broke eye contact as he looked down at his yellow tablet and picked up his pen as if to take notes. He thought to himself, *As a news man, what can I learn from this enemy? I need a quick question so the Russian will show his true colors.*

Zachar sat down. "Mr. Cannon, the American people will

need Eagle News more than you know. They must hear the truth from you, and the others. They are afraid, but the truth will comfort them."

Cannon straightened up as if he had heard exactly what he needed to hear, and looked his enemy in the eye. "You're right. They deserve the truth and that's the only thing they're going to get from Eagle News and me."

Zachar smirked. *Cannon is about to go to work on me.*

Cannon lit into Zachar with his first direct question. "Is it true that Russian forces secretly and cowardly, unprovoked, attacked the United States of America today?"

Zachar held eye contact with Cannon and said, "Yes, that is true, except not cowardly. It took a lot of courage on our part."

"Is it true that as we speak, the Russian Navy is steaming across the Atlantic to invade America?"

"Yes, that is also true. The first ships will be here the day after tomorrow."

"So it's true that the United States and Russia are at war!"

"No, that's not true," Zachar answered quickly. "Neither side has declared war. We are not here to destroy America but to take her over. In fact, my government intends to disarm and displace the present central government with one of our own."

Cannon stared at him. "Do you really think the American people are just going to lie down and let your army run over them without a fight?"

Zachar looked confident as he explained, "Not exactly. Our fight is with your military, not with your civilian population."

"And you think your armies will march across this land after our military, the different states' national guards, plus a great militia of armed citizens, and they are not going to fight you every step of the way?"

"Sure. We know there will be some resistance. That is to be expected. We are prepared for that."

Cannon thought to himself, *This man is crazy or he knows something we don't.* Then aloud he asked, "What kind of bomb or missile was used to destroy the Pentagon?"

"Well, Mr. Cannon, I believe we will leave that up to your scientists and bomb makers to try and figure out on their own."

Cannon again thought to himself, *It didn't hurt to ask. Let's try another question.* He took a quick breath. "How many Russian submarines are there off the East Coast?"

Zachar smiled and shook his head. "No, Mr. Cannon. You really wouldn't want to know that. If you were to give that kind of information in your broadcast, well, let me put it this way: the military are also monitoring all of the news from this place, and before you and I could get out of this building..." He paused to let that sink in. "I believe you and I, and your New York neighbors I spoke of earlier, would wish you had never said that. Be careful what you ask and what you say. Our lives, as well as many others depend upon it." Zachar shifted in his chair. "Troop strengths, directions, and locations of armed forces... I'm sure neither side would like that kind of information to be broadcast."

Zachar stood up. "Our interview is over but, Mr. Cannon, the answer to many of your questions can be found from your state governors and city or town mayors."

"What do you mean?" Cannon asked, puzzled.

Zachar looked at Cannon and said, "At 12 noon today, every state governor and city mayor received vital information about how they must govern their state, city, and town to continue to have their freedom and to avoid a national tragedy."

Cannon stared at Zachar. "Again, what do you mean?"

Zachar smiled. "I have just given you an important

piece of information. I cannot do your job for you. You are news people. Go find out. That is what you do, is it not? Check out information? It will be extremely important to the people to have that news." Zachar walked toward the door, "I'll be in the control room if you need me."

"But I have more questions," Cannon said.

"I am sure you do, but that is all you get from me today," Zachar stated as he walked out the door, leaving behind a frustrated Wayne Cannon.

The Eagle management set up three groups to work 24/7 verifying stories and reports to make sure they were accurate and would not cause Eagle News any problems. All live interviews were held back at least 30 minutes to make certain the person being interviewed, or the reporter doing the interview, did not say something they could not broadcast. Of course, if anything were to be said, it would be edited out. Exactly as Zachar predicted, there were several New York police and National Guard soldiers with trucks around the building, and at the Russian embassy.

On the West Coast in Eugene, Oregon, Brad Wilson, his family, and many other members, were at the church building all afternoon talking and praying for the congregation, the nation, its military, and the nation's leaders. They asked God to give the leaders wisdom, ability, and opportunity to lead the nation as He would have them to. They also asked God to protect the nation and its people from their enemies.

A young woman who had just arrived at the building came in and said, "On my way here I heard an announcement over the radio. They said several times that at 8 p.m. Eastern Standard Time there's going to be a special report regarding news about the war. Everyone is being told to tune in to listen or watch the broadcast."

Upon hearing this, the men gathered and talked about what could happen regarding the national situation. The ladies went to a room across the hall to pray, not only for their own families, but for all families in the nation. At 10 minutes before 8 p.m. EST they all gathered in front of a television.

In New York City, as Wayne Cannon prepared his broadcast, he was concerned because he had been given no instructions from the government. All he could do or say was what he had learned from reports that had come in from across the country. He felt it would have been better for some leader, like the President, to address the people on the news rather than himself on a news broadcast. Since there was no other way, he began. "As I stand before you tonight, I do so with a broken heart for our nation, which today has been under heavy attack for more than nine hours. It is a secret, unprovoked attack against our nation, government, and military. On behalf of this great nation I ask for God's help."

As he spoke, video clips of the day's events were played on a large monitor behind him. "The Russian government is behind it, and the losses of our brave men and women in the military are tremendous. As a nation we must expect an invasion within a few days. All of our national government leadership have moved from Washington, D.C. to some secret location. There, we believe, they will reorganize our military and our national resources to withstand our enemy's future actions."

Cannon paused a few seconds and looked down at his notes. He was reluctant to go forward with the news. He took a deep breath, exhaled, and went on. "We as Americans hold our allegiance to the United States of America, our Constitution, and our duly-elected government. But we learned earlier today that every state governor and most city and town mayors this side of the Rocky Mountains have received written information from the Russian government. Eagle News has talked with many of these governors and mayors to confirm that this communication has in fact been delivered to them."

After another deep breath and slight pause, Cannon said, "I can report to you tonight that all of whom we talked with

confirmed that Russian forces intend to invade this country in a few days. However, they have no intention of attacking the American people, her cities, or assets. Their conflict will only involve the central government and its military. They intend to hold each state government solely responsible for their own state and that state's actions in this takeover. Likewise, all city governments will be held responsible for the control of their people and their assets. The invasion forces will cross this country and will do their best to avoid highly populated areas as they pursue the central government and the military. The people of each state and city can remain safe and may use their National Guard units and police forces to keep civil peace and order in their jurisdictions. Every effort will be made not to destroy your power and water supplies. You will have the ability to continue to conduct commerce in your state with safety, as long as it does not interfere with military movements on either side."

Cannon's anger began to seep through. He struggled to maintain composure. When he spoke again, his words were distinct. "We were also informed that no air travel of any kind will be permitted, and that any aircraft will be shot down without warning. This will begin in sixteen hours from now. Each state and city was informed that if the invasion is resisted by any state by the use of its National Guard, police, or any militia against the Russian military, that state and its main cities will immediately be destroyed in the same manner as was the Pentagon, losing all its power, water supplies, and communications.

"I will give you a moment to think about what I have just said because there is more." Cannon stood motionless a full minute then he said, "All resistance from the U.S. military will be met as if in war. Any military personnel who are killed or wounded will be turned over to the state where the action occurred. The state then will be responsible for proper military funerals, as well as for treatment of the sick and wounded. All American military personnel will be treated as the brave men and women they are, with dignity and respect."

Again, Cannon paused to look at his notes before going on. "Any non-U.S. military of any kind who attack or in any way hinder the invading forces will be dealt with in ways that will not be described here. That includes National Guard, militia groups, gangs, or individuals. Absolutely no prisoners will be taken except for U.S. military."

Cannon again paused from his broadcast and stood visibly straighter. Changing his tone, he said, "My fellow Americans, these are truly the most desperate times our nation has ever experienced. We are a people who have never backed down from a fight, and tonight I want to say to you that we cannot lose heart. God help us all and God bless America." As the program ended, the American flag filled the screen, and "God Bless America" played in the background.

As soon as Cannon received the signal that he was off the air, he stood up, grabbed his laptop, and slung it across the room, hitting one of the monitors. Spider-web cracks filled the screen as it went black.

Cannon stomped out of the studio and down the hall into the control room. As he crossed the room, people stood to watch him. Shoving chairs and tables out of his way, he headed straight for Zachar who had stood up when he saw Cannon enter the room.

One of his agents raised and chambered his weapon. Zachar put out his hand toward him and said, "It is alright. I will take care of this. Our American friend seems upset."

Cannon stopped directly in front of Zachar balling his fists at his sides. "You...! You used me to do your dirty work!"

Zachar pointed a finger in his face. "Mr. Cannon, this is war."

"I don't care what you call it! You will never use me again!" Cannon yelled. He turned and stomped away. A few other people in the room went after him.

Zachar crossed his arms with a smile. "Oh yes I will, because you are an excellent news man."

Out in the hallway the men who had followed Cannon were trying to calm him down.

"Wayne, you can't do stuff like that," one man told him urgently. "You're risking all of our lives. We don't want to make Zachar angry."

Cannon blurted out, "He used me to put fear in the hearts of our viewers and to take away their will to rebel against our invaders."

Another man said, "That's true, but the governors and the mayors wanted it reported so the people could know how they can stay safe."

The other man said, "Wayne, you had no choice. The people had to know."

Cannon's shoulders slumped as he reluctantly replied, "I know they had to know, but I didn't have to be the one to tell them." They all knew Cannon had simply reported the truth, but in doing so, had helped the Russians place great fear in the hearts of the American people.

Jesus answered, "You could have no power at all against Me unless it had been given you from above." -John 19:11a

For the kingdom is the Lord's, And He rules over the nations. -Psalm 22:28

CHAPTER 6

THE WAR-TIME SECRET

Two days later, shortly before 5 a.m., the Morning Eagles show was about to start in Studio A. The hosts were anchorman Randy Wade with co-hosts Judy Best and Steve Harmon. The three of them stood with their backs to the camera, looking out the large glass windows.

The morning light of a new day streamed through the canyons in the great city of New York. People darted here and there on the street without speaking to those they met. Police and emergency-vehicle sirens could be heard, their blinking emergency lights flashing as they crossed the boulevard. Groups of New York National Guard trucks and other armored cars drove by. The newscasters watched the scene in silence.

Word came in their earpieces, "One minute. Take your places."

The three readied themselves, knowing the program would not begin with good news today, nor many days to come. They settled themselves on the curved couch as the opening credits appeared to the viewers with a new graphic entitled, "Our Nation Under Siege."

Randy Wade began the broadcast. "There is so much news to bring you that we are changing the format. The three of us will report stories as they come into the newsroom. I'll begin by telling you that since Wayne Cannon spoke to the nation last night, these are some of the things we know: every state government in the East has called up their National Guard,

and most states have given their State Police special war-time powers much like a state military police. Every state, and most large cities, have established martial law overnight. These laws require mandatory curfews from sunset to sunrise. Most all cities have given their police widespread power to deal with crime and criminals, especially any citizen who attacks police or other officials with deadly force."

Judy spoke next. "We have received thousands of reports throughout the night of rioting and looting throughout all the major cities in the East."

"What are they rioting about?" Harmon asked.

Judy replied, "Some riots are because they are demanding that the government protect them. Some are against martial law and curfews." She paused, then continued, "They seem to think this allows them to break into any business they want, stealing and looting as they go. They seem to be targeting food and drug stores. Early this morning in a few of the cities, the police were given the go-ahead to shoot looters coming out of stores with stolen items. It's like some people believe they have a right to what other people have because of this national emergency." Suddenly, Judy stopped for a second, looked at her iPad, then back at the camera. "I have just been told that the death toll overnight could be as high as fifteen thousand people killed in all the major cities east of Chicago." Tears filled her eyes as she said in a quivering voice, "This is crazy! We are killing ourselves!"

Harmon picked up with his report. He looked at his iPad, touched his earpiece, then said, "Overnight, all of the United States airlines have flown their aircraft west beyond the Rocky Mountains. Most all foreign aircraft have gone north to Canada, with some going to South America. None are going east. The airlines are carrying extra pilots, maintenance and repair people, airline executives, and as many employees and their families as they can. It's reported that all private aircraft are out West."

As the Morning Eagles closed their broadcast, they too

asked everyone to pray for the nation, the leaders, the military, and all of the police and families who lost their lives in the riots overnight. The program closed with the American flag flying and a choral group singing "God Bless America."

The broadcast switched to the news deck in Studio C with Bill Sawyer and Frank Summers. Sawyer came on after the breaking news graphic. "Frank and I will be bringing you the mid-morning news on this second day of the assault on our nation. We must report that a large part of this great nation has been thrown into turmoil and despair. As daylight spreads across the East, we can only begin to tell about, and show, some of the video that has come to us in the aftermath of night-long riots in most of our large cities. The worst places are littered with bodies, like a war zone. Hospitals are reporting many wounded. They are only able to treat the most severe wounds."

The camera switched to Summers, standing next to a large wall monitor. He began with a warning. "What I am about to show you, you may not want to see. You definitely do not want your children to see this. Our newsroom is receiving thousands of similar reports from all over." Summers stopped and looked down wishing he didn't have to say the words he was about to speak. Instead, he braced himself and turned back to the camera. "These reports are coming from all over. Thousands of suicides have been reported. The police say there could be as many as fifty thousand in one night. Some officials are reporting countless more murder-suicides of families. One expert predicts that over the next few days there could be as many as two-hundred thousand suicides." The videos matched the warning Summers had given. Horrid war-like scenes flashed on the screen over and over. Summers ended his report with, "None of us would have ever imagined such scenes taking place on American soil. Pray for our country."

At 11 a.m. EST Sawyer and Summers stopped their various news reports. Sawyer said, "Ladies and gentlemen. We are now going to pause with our nation to remember that only twenty-four hours ago the first missile hit the Pentagon in Washington, D.C. We will have a moment of silence for all who

lost loved ones in this vicious, unprovoked attack on our military yesterday."

At 12 noon, Bart Hamilton and Brad Lucas took over the afternoon news in front of the graphic, "Our Nation Under Siege." As the song "God Bless America" played, there was a sudden, deafening roar of Russian fighter jets over the city. They flew low and fast just above the buildings. They came in from the east going west, and in less than 10 minutes the planes turned and crossed back over the city again, going east out over the Atlantic Ocean. Within minutes, Eagle News had reports of Russian planes also flying over cities from Boston, Massachusetts to Norfolk, Virginia, and then more reports from as far south as Jacksonville, Florida. They left as quickly as they came.

As the planes flew over New York City, Hamilton found someone in the studio who had knowledge of what was going on. Hamilton stood beside the man and said, "With us now is Air Force Colonel Leon Morris, Retired, one of the Eagle News producers." Hamilton then asked, "What do you make of these hundreds of Russian planes flying over us and then leaving?"

Colonel Morris said, "First of all, I believe they wanted to scare us, to show they were close enough to get to us if they wanted to."

"Are there carriers just off the coast?"

"No. I think it tells us those Russian carriers are still a ways off, but they wanted us to know they are getting closer."

"How close do you think they are?"

"I would guess in two days we could see those carriers on the horizon." Colonel Morris went on to say, "They have warned us not to have any aircraft flying after noon today. I'm sure they want us to know they can do what they said they could and take down our civilian air fleet. If they can fly over New York today, in less than two days they could be hitting targets as far west as Chicago. If they were to get a carrier or two in the Gulf of Mexico off of Texas, they could reach as far as Denver."

"What about our Air Force?" Hamilton asked.

Colonel Morris sighed and said, "Bart, I'll tell you this. The Russians targeted the Air Force with most of those special attack missiles. I believe they did so because they are afraid of our Air Force. But from all reports, they did a job on us. There is no Air Force this side of Kansas City. And what was from there to Denver has moved west beyond the Rockies." He hesitated then continued, "What's left is now reorganizing and planning. You can count on it."

The impromptu interview ended and Lucas was back on with his guest, Eric Ford, who headed up the financial news from the Eagle Business channel. Lucas asked, "Can you tell us what is happening on Wall Street?"

"Within an hour after the attack, the New York Stock Exchange shut down and has stayed down, freezing all stock, prices, and sales worldwide," Ford responded. "All other world exchanges have also stopped trading in U.S. stocks. The U.S. dollar is dropping like a rock in value on the world markets."

"Do you have any idea as to what is going to happen to the country financially?"

Ford replied, "Brad, it doesn't look good now, but it's too early to know. Until things change, the stock market, I'm sure, will stay closed to keep us from a financial collapse. Also, all of the banks are closed and will probably stay closed until we know more. It's important that they keep the banks from having a run on them. Hopefully, each state will get the banks back open a few hours a day so businesses can continue to function. I understand the state governments are meeting with banks to work out a way to keep the economy from collapsing."

Lucas asked, "If the dollars are not good, will people who have gold be better off?"

Ford responded quickly, "No, not at all. If you have a can of gold coins buried in your backyard you can take them down to Wal-Mart, but I don't believe they're going to sell you a loaf of bread and a gallon of milk for one of those coins. First, neither you nor they know if the coin is worth the bread and milk. The large grocery chains have no way to deal in gold and probably couldn't for a long time. The American dollar will be beaten down, but in the long run, we will be able to continue to use it. And let's pray that we're not going to have to start using rubles."

"How bad do you think it will be?"

"All we know is the Russians have told us they do not want to destroy the nation or its economy. All I know is that it's going to be bad until we learn more of what is going to happen in the weeks to come."

Henry King, long time Eagle White House reporter, left Washington, D.C. with the government and was some place in the west. He sent a message via his friend, Robert Marshale.

At 5:50 p.m. Robert Marshale and his wife walked into the Eagle building, having just arrived in New York from D.C. He sought out someone he knew and asked them if they could arrange a meeting with himself and Roger Foster, preferably where they could not be heard. Shortly, Marshale and Foster met in the computer server room hoping they could not be overheard because of computer fan noise. Everyone suspected the Russians had bugged many of the rooms in the building.

After their meeting, Foster and Marshale went to the office where Wayne Cannon and staff were having their meeting in preparation for Cannon's program at 8 p.m. When they entered the room, Foster held up a sheet of paper that read, "Keep on with your meeting. Don't talk to us."

The two men sat down at the table with the others. Foster sat next to Cannon and slid him a note.

Marshale got a message from Henry King. He's with the president but couldn't say where. President told him to tell the people he and staff are safe. Preparing to get our military ready to defend our nation soon.

As Cannon read the note and passed it on to the producers at the table, Foster wrote a second note. Cannon and his producers continued talking about the night's broadcast.

Foster slid the second note in front of Cannon. Cannon looked at Marshale, sensing that Marshale wanted to see the expression on his face when he read it. He looked down and read:

Chinese coming to help defeat Russians. President met at Chinese Consulate in San Francisco. Chinese sending troops. Navy made up of American ships we gave them. Their Air Force also has our fighter planes. Promised to bring everything except what's needed at their northern border. Chinese have loaned US $3 trill to pay for civilian food.

Cannon's face broke into a big smile as he looked up from the note and looked at Marshale, still watching him. Cannon passed the note on to the others and picked up his pen. He scribbled hurriedly and held up his notepad for everyone in the room to see.

NO NEWS BROADCAST ABOUT CHINESE. WAR-TIME SECRET GIVE-AWAY TO RUSSIANS.

Marshale leaned across the table and whispered to Cannon, "The Russians have spies everywhere. They will know when the Chinese troops show up."

Cannon quickly scratched out another note.

NO ONE CAN HEAR THIS FROM US.

Cannon looked at all who were sitting around the table. Everyone agreed that this was wonderful news for the people, but it would betray the nation's plans. The 8 o'clock news was not going to be so true and reliable after all.

In Eugene, Oregon, on the third day of war, Brad was in his office with only a few of his employees. They were helping close down the business. No one was interested in buying a house, even houses under construction. No one wanted to buy under war conditions. Most contracts had cancelled because the banks were closed, and no one knew what was going to happen.

Brad's phone rang. He looked and saw his brother-in-law's name, Ken Lloyd. Ken was the man in charge of all the air traffic controllers in the Seattle–Tacoma International Airport and all air traffic in the northwest part of Washington state. Brad answered on the second ring. "Hey, Ken! What's going on up there with you? How are Sarah and the kids?"

Ken's response was quick. "Well, that's what I'm calling about. Do you have a vacant house that Sarah and the kids could use?"

"Sure I do," Brad answered. "What's going on?"

"I want to send the family down there with you for the time being. I believe Seattle has just become Russia's next biggest target."

"Why do you think that?"

"Brad, this is not public news yet but it will be in a few days. The Chinese are coming. The U.S. government has asked them to bring their military forces and equipment to help defend us against the Russians."

"But that's great news, Ken," Brad said. "Maybe that's the answer to our prayers!"

Ken continued, "We were just told in a meeting to be ready. The Chinese will get every ship that will float and load it with men and equipment to arrive in Seattle, San Francisco, and Los Angeles. The American government has also war-leased every plane in the U.S. commercial airlines, most of which are here in the west. We were told that these planes would be used to fly Chinese troops from China to the U.S. And here in Seattle, we should be expecting as many as five hundred flights per day. Also, FedEx and UPS planes will be flying equipment and supplies into Portland and San Francisco."

"That's great news," Brad repeated. "I'll head up to Portland to be there when Sarah and the kids arrive."

"Okay," said Ken. "I think I can get them out of here in a few hours." Then as if interrupted, Ken said, "I gotta go. Give my love to Carol and the kids and keep us all in your prayers."

"For sure. We'll do that and you take care," Brad said and hung up.

At 5:30 p.m. EST, that same day, Nancy Coleman was reporting in the Eagle News studios. She stopped mid-sentence, put her hand to her earpiece and waited. After a few seconds she spoke. "We are going to a special report from Isidro Morales, where he is embedded with the Russian military in an unknown place. Isidro, are you there?"

The TV screen reflected a bad signal, coming in and going out for a few seconds. The signal cleared a bit and Isidro appeared, but only enough to barely make him out. Nancy said, "Can you tell us where you are?"

"No," he said. "Not exactly. I can tell you that I'm on the deck of a Russian aircraft carrier in the Atlantic. We've been here about four hours. I can also tell you that behind Carl, my camera man, are two well-armed soldiers and a translator, listening to my every word. I've been given a lot of freedom to go about the ship almost anywhere I want. Of course, the armed guards never let us out of their sight, and I had to tell them what I was going to report to you tonight. I'm surprised that there are very few things I can't say. So here goes with what I can tell you and show you, and what I've seen and heard. I can't show you, but I can tell you that looking north or south from the flight deck of this carrier, there are ships of every kind all the way to the horizon. The carrier has slowed in the last couple of hours,

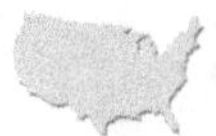

waiting for other ships behind us to catch up. And if you were to look behind us to the east, you would see many more ships. Some are troop ships. I could see soldiers on the deck. There are large supply ships. One supply ship had a big, black submarine on each side of her. It looked like they were reloading the subs. The decks of the submarine were like a beehive around the missile launch openings. The missiles looked like those launched against us a few days ago. I also saw a large ship like I've never seen before. It has much larger missiles. I was told that I'd be able to go ashore with the army in the next day or two, so we must be getting close to the United States. From what little I have been able to learn from speaking with some of the Russian officers who speak some English, it seems as if being here, off the coast of the U.S., was a surprise to them. They thought they were going to be off the coast of China this week. I think attacking America is big news, even to these Russian sailors. Everyone's morale seems high, and it appears that everyone is well equipped." Isidro paused then said, "I have to go now. I hope we're getting ready for this. Tell everyone at the Eagle that if I don't see them again, it's been good."

The camera went back to Nancy. "Be safe my friend, Isidro," she said, then continued her newscast. "It will be nightfall here in the East in a couple of hours. We have been told that most all state, city, and county police are reminding everyone about the dusk to dawn curfew except for emergency workers. The police, in most places, are broadcasting over the local radio and television stations that there is no tolerance. Looters would be shot on sight, as will anyone who attacks the police or National Guard." She paused. "We are receiving continuous reports of millions of people on the highways going west. Some highways are blocked with people who have run out of gas and are just walking. The roadsides are littered with abandoned cars. In some states, to keep the highways clear, workers with bulldozers are pushing cars off the roadway. These people appear to be either older people, or those with young families trying to find a safer place. It's also reported that thousands of people are trying to cross our northern border into Canada. The Canadians are trying to stop them because they cannot care for that many people's needs. And if they are there this winter, many more will die without shelter."

Nancy moved to a big wall screen with pictures from various locations, but mostly helicopters and tops of buildings. She said, "The biggest exodus of people are those moving south across the Texas border into Mexico. They have been asked why they are fleeing. The answers are all the same. They think there will be a great war. At the border, the Mexican military were trying to keep people from crossing the river, and were shooting men, women, and children as they crossed. There were so many people they overran the Mexican soldiers. Many of them were killed by other people crossing and stampeding. Every highway crossing Texas is completely filled with people heading south. We are told that New Mexico, Arizona, and California borders are also packed with people trying to get out. Experts say this is the greatest migration of people ever seen across the world in modern times. Governments of South America are trying to stop the migration into their countries as well because they won't have food or money to care for them."

At noon on the fourth day, Shirley Steele and Connie Cooper teamed up to cover the next four hours of news at Eagle. They had been gone for a couple of days to make sure their families were in a safe place, and were now back to do what they could to get true, factual news to the people of America.

Connie began the news. "Reports are coming to us from all the governors and mayors, telling us all they can do is to contain gangs and looters in various areas at night. Many gangs are warring with each other over drugs, which are now in very low supply. Last night in Chicago alone, the police estimated over 2,000 people were killed. Because of this nightly crime spree, more and more people are fleeing the big cities. Some people say that they are more afraid of gangs and looters than they are of the Russian armies." Connie stopped, raised both eyebrows, then said, "Wal-Mart is trying to hire up to twenty thousand armed security personnel, nationwide, to protect their stores, warehouses, and trucks. Many other food store chains are also trying to hire people for protection."

The camera turned to Shirley Steele as she began her report in front of a graphic that read "SPECIAL REPORT." "We are also receiving reports from Europe. The French especially, but other European countries as well, are trying to keep from being overrun by their Muslim population. Some large cities there seem to be close to civil war." Shirley took a breath, then went on. "We've also received reports from South Korea that the North Koreans are amassing a great army at their border. They are expecting an invasion at any time. In the Middle East, North Africa, and Asia, Muslims are taking advantage of the invasion there to also try to take over those local governments." Shirley paused with her hand to her earpiece then continued, "I've just gotten word that we are in contact with John Walton, former U.S. ambassador to the United Nations."

John Walton's face appeared on a screen beside Shirley, and she asked, "Ambassador Walton, with the U.S. invasion by the Russians and all of the other things going on around the world, tell us what the UN is doing about these situations."

The Ambassador shook his head. "There is no UN, Shirley. By the second day every single one of them had run away like rats jumping off a burning ship." The Ambassador kept shaking his head. "I don't believe we are likely to see a UN anywhere anytime soon."

A "BREAKING NEWS" graphic appeared on the screen. The camera turned to Connie, who was visibly upset. "Something has gone terribly wrong. Reports are now coming in that some type of enemy weapon has hit the city of Galveston, Texas. Early reports from people in the suburbs of the city are saying there is now no city." She hesitated, then asked, "Is this a part of the invasion? I thought the Russians had told us that no harm would come to the civilian population. Did they lie, or what's going on? We will come back to this story as soon as we know more."

In the control room, Roger Foster, president of Eagle News, and four program producers angrily approached Zachar, who was in his usual place overseeing the control room. Mr.

Foster spoke in anger. "You lied to us. What happened in Galveston?"

Zachar said calmly, "I warned you. The military are monitoring all types of broadcasts. Your own people here in this room know why this happened."

"What do you mean 'our people know?'" one of the producers questioned.

Zachar responded, "You are news people. Go find out for yourself."

The men turned and walked as a determined group to where those who were responsible for checking stories and reports were hastily working. Mr. Foster asked the group in general, "Do you know what happened in Galveston?"

"Yes sir," a man in the middle of the group spoke up. "There was a video from the Galveston station KTVC with a report they had received from an oil rig helicopter. They had broadcast the video to us and everyone they could. It showed an aircraft carrier and one of those big black subs plus two other ships. They went on to provide the latitude and longitude of their location with the speed and direction they were going. We saw it, but we knew we could not broadcast that kind of information. We didn't say anything; we just hoped they'd get away with it. They sent it to others in the West as well. Perhaps they were hoping our military could use the information."

One of the producers solemnly said, "I'm sorry, but they did what all of us were told we could not do."

At 5:30 a.m. on the morning of the sixth day, from Studio A at Eagle News, the Morning Eagles show began with an "ALERT" graphic followed by the words, "Our Nation Under Siege." Randy Wade, the news co-anchor and best-selling author, announced, "We are now going live to a report from David Wade." Randy Wade, David's father, asked, "David, are you okay?

No one here has heard from you in almost twenty-four hours."

"I'm okay," David assured his dad. "We've been traveling on a lot of back roads that are very congested and it's hard to find fuel. We were stopped several times, mostly in small towns, by people who wanted to know who we were and what we were doing."

"Son, I hope you're very careful out there."

David replied quickly, "Dad, I'm okay. Tell Mom I'm okay and that I send my love. We are being very careful."

Judy Best broke in and asked, "David, can you tell us where you are?"

"No, Judy. We can't say on the air where we are. I can tell you that we are on the coast at a place where ship after ship has been unloading Russian troops and equipment all night. And we can't show video because it may give away where we are." David paused a second. "I can tell you that from where we are, we can see their army has moved inland over two hundred miles in the night. Now that it's daylight, we can look out and see a long line of large ships waiting to get into the unloading areas. We can also see a larger carrier on the horizon, and overhead there are Russian helicopters and fighter planes patrolling the army. We are sure this must be the invasion."

Steve Harmon asked, "Have you seen or heard any resistance to the invasion?"

"No, sunrise was only 30 minutes ago. Yesterday and last night, we saw a lot of men on the road, mostly in pick-ups carrying guns, but we did not see any organized resistance like a National Guard unit."

Judy looked at her iPad and said, "Eagle News has been able to confirm three locations along the east coast much like what David just told us about."

Later in the morning, about 9:30 a.m., Bill Sawyer and Connie Cooper took over the Eagle's morning news. Connie said,

"Let me show you an article from the front page of the Wall Street Journal. It reads, 'Many religious leaders signed and sent this to the President and the Congress, requesting they declare this coming Saturday and Sunday to be set aside for two days of prayer and fasting for the nation. They asked the President to come on national TV and lead the nation in the first prayer of each day. They also asked the government to publicly repent of all sins of this great and godly nation, to ask God's forgiveness for us as people, and for His help in our time of need, in the name of our Lord and Savior Jesus Christ.' Also printed in the article was the President's reply, 'As the President of the greatest nation on earth, I will not belittle myself or this country before the eyes of the world as if we have done anything wrong. Besides, this kind of public display would be an insult to this nation's atheists, Jews, and Muslims. The people of America must trust in their government and in our military to defeat our enemies. This is the greatest nation on earth with the strongest military in the world.'"

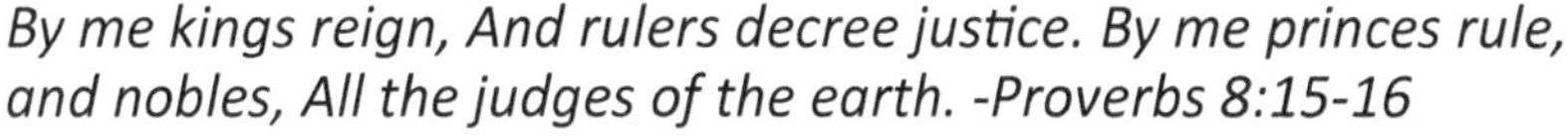

By me kings reign, And rulers decree justice. By me princes rule, and nobles, All the judges of the earth. -Proverbs 8:15-16

"You have heard that it was said, 'You shall love your neighbor and hate your enemy.' But I say to you, love your enemies, bless those who curse you, do good to those who hate you, and pray for those who spitefully use you and persecute you, that you may be sons of your Father in heaven; for He makes His sun rise on the evil and on the good, and sends rain on the just and on the unjust." -Matthew 5:43-45

CHAPTER 7

THE MESSAGE

At 11 a.m. the next morning Eric Ford, anchor and business journalist for Eagle News, walked towards the television station's building from a hotel two blocks away, where some of the Eagle employees and families were housed for convenience and safety. As he stopped and waited for the traffic light to change, a middle-aged woman walked up to his left side and stood close beside him.

The woman looked straight ahead but spoke just loud enough for him to hear. "My husband is General Don McKay. He wants you to give this to Mr. Blackburn."

Ford turned his eyes downward and spied an envelope she held close to her right elbow. Ford took the envelope from her and placed it in his pocket. The light changed and he and the group of people waiting together crossed the street. As Ford stepped onto the opposite sidewalk, the woman spoke in a loud voice across the intersection, "It is urgent." Then she turned and walked back the way she had come.

At the office he approached the receptionist. "I need to see Mr. Blackburn."

"Mr. Blackburn has gone for the day," she replied.

Ford knew it was important. He looked at the envelope. It was not sealed and there was no name on the outside. He opened the envelope, took out the note and read it.

Eagle News, I am General McKay. I am here in New York

City from the western war department in Denver, Colorado. I have information for you from the President. I think I am being followed. I have left the hotel where my wife is. I am at the Biltmore on 38th Street. Room 622. I will be there from 1 p.m. to 2 p.m. Then I must leave. Send people whom I will recognize from TV so that I will know to whom I am talking. 1 P.M. TODAY. DO NOT BE FOLLOWED.

Ford looked at the clock. He had less than two hours to find some people the General would know and get them to the hotel a half a mile away with no one following them. He went over to the news division where he found Brad Lucas and Frank Summers. He showed each of them the note. They both agreed to meet on the 6th floor of the hotel.

At 12:55 the three men, who had traveled different ways to get to the hotel, met again on the 6th floor, went to room 622, and knocked. General McKay opened the door and looked at each man carefully. He immediately recognized them from Eagle News and motioned them to come in. He quickly glanced both ways down the hall and closed the door. As the four men moved into the room, the General went to a table and poured himself a drink. It was obvious this was not his first drink. He motioned to them to help themselves but they said in unison, "No thanks. We're working."

Ford spoke first. "Your note said you have a message from the President."

"Yes, I do," the General replied. "The President wants you to know that he intends to address the nation on the 15th and he wants you to carry the broadcast and his message to the nation."

Summers asked, "General, will he know that he's on a 30-minute delay and will be cut off if what he says will endanger us and a big part of this city?"

"He knows," said the General. "He wants you to get him clearance for a live broadcast."

Lucas asked, "General, do you know what he's going to talk about?"

"Yes. He is going to declare war against Russia."

Ford seemed puzzled. "General, why didn't the President declare war on the very first day?"

The General took a long drink to finish his glass. "The President had to wait until the Chinese were able to get over here to help us."

Lucas spoke up again, "General, I think you know some things that we don't know and if you want us to help, you're going to have to tell us why we should help."

Summers added, "That's right, General. You want our help; tell us why he's waited so long."

Ford asked, "Where is our military and why haven't they attacked the invading armies?"

The General looked at each man. They knew the retired General had had too much to drink, but they were also aware that he knew some big secrets they needed to get out of him. The General again filled his glass over halfway and sat down in one of the chairs. Then he blurted out, "Nothing has gone good for us. We lost most of our best and brightest leaders at the Pentagon. Then the surprise missile attack was so well done that we lost over half of all military in the east. And for over twenty years, we had been warning the government not to convert our military into paid civilian subcontractors, but they have done that with almost half the job positions. After the attacks, it became obvious the government would not have money to pay the civilian contractors, so they simply quit, and went home. History has taught us over and over that paid armies only work in good times." He repeated, "They simply walked away. They said they came to work, not to fight," He hesitated.

Ford sensed there was more. "General, you're not telling us everything."

The General looked again at each one of them and took another drink before going on. "No, it's worse than that. For almost fifteen years, the government has been filling the ranks of our military by offering every illegal alien the chance to enlist in our military for four years or more. After four years they would automatically become U.S. citizens. Again, we warned the government. Now, knowing their life is not worth a piece of paper to make them citizens, most of them are headed to some border out of this country."

Summers asked, "What about our own volunteer military?"

The General straightened with pride and said, "Those brave men and women are the real military; they won't back down from anything. There's not a coward among them! And they are the ones the Russians are afraid of, that's for sure. They were ready to go by the second day. But the Army has been reduced over the years and now there are not enough of them. Right now, most of them are bogged down on the west side of the Dakotas. There are also units in Nebraska, Kansas, and Oklahoma." He stopped to take another drink. "But there is also a wall of people blocking every major highway moving west and southwest. If they were told to go today, I'm not sure how they could do it."

Ford asked, "Are you saying there's no hope?"

"No, but we can't do it without the Chinese," the General answered. "Ten thousand Chinese troops come in by air every day. In a few days, hundreds of supply ships and transport ships will be docking on the West Coast. Soon, a 250,000-man army, who have all our latest equipment by the way, will establish a military front along the east side of the Rockies. That is why the President wants to tell the people on the 15th. Then they will be ready to move east. The Chinese Air Force has been flying in, in all of those new fighter jets we gave them, and will back up our Air Force."

Ford asked, "What about our Navy?"

The General took another drink and said, "This is another secret." He stopped and looked each man in the eye. "All United States naval ships in the world are making their way to a secret rendezvous in the South Atlantic so they can come up behind the Russian Navy." The General looked at his watch and said, "It's 2 o'clock now. I have to go. I better leave first. Each of you better leave at different times through different doors." The General took his coat and bottle and left.

Once back at the Eagle News offices, Frank Summers went straight to one of the Eagle managers, and together they went to meet with the people assigned to verify all reports for broadcasting. After he explained what was needed, Summers, the supervisor, and the clearance people went to meet with Zachar.

The supervisor spoke first. "One of our reporters has informed us that our President wants to address the nation at 8 p.m. EST on the 15th."

Zachar looked at Summers. "What is this about?"

Summers, not wanting to give too much information, said, "I do not wish to speak for the President."

Zachar smiled. "But you know what he wants to do, don't you? Do you think he wants to tell the people that he intends to declare war on us?" Zachar's smile disappeared. He looked hard at Frank Summers. "Or maybe he wants to tell everyone to attack our armies. Could it be that he wants to warn the nation as to our locations?" Zachar leaned towards Summers. "Maybe he wants to tell the people that there are tens of thousands of Chinese who have come to help him and now he's ready to fight."

The men didn't know what to say to Zachar. The Chinese had been a secret. Nothing public had been said.

Zachar said, "He is still the President of your great nation and has the honor, and right, to address his people."

The supervisor spoke again. "The President wants to speak live without the 30-minute delay."

Zachar again looked hard at each man, then said, "Live?" He paused. "The best I can give you is a two-minute delay, and I will hold the button to cut him off." Zachar smiled again, "I do not want to be here with you. If the President says something wrong, that could get us all killed in this place."

The men from Eagle News now had the permission they needed, and from that hour on until the 15th, Eagle would make a public announcement every hour for the upcoming message from the President.

At 10:15 a.m. EST on the 9th day at Eagle News, Bill Sawyer and Bart Hamilton were holding down the mid-morning broadcast. Sawyer said, "We are receiving a special report from Isidro Morales, one of our Eagle reporters, traveling with the Russian army." Morales appeared on a large monitor next to Sawyer. "Can you tell us where you are today?"

"Yes, I can. The Russian information officer from whom I must get an 'OK' on what I say, has told me that as of today, I can tell you where we are. The army I'm with is now stopped on I-40 at Memphis, Tennessee. We've been at a standstill since midnight. I'm about fifteen miles back from the lead unit. They were waiting until daylight to give the forwarding units a chance to recheck the bridge that goes over the Mississippi River. I was also told that the other two armies are stopped at the Mississippi, one at Vicksburg, and the other in St. Louis, Missouri. They are planning for all three armies to cross the river before noon today."

Sawyer asked, "How dangerous has it been traveling near the front of the army?"

Morales hesitated before he answered. "The unit I'm riding in has been hit with more bullets than I have ever seen in all of my war reporting. It's very dangerous. Men are losing their lives on both sides. I'm in unit five. There are ten units in the army. Each unit will take a turn at the front for about an hour, then we stop and rest and get additional ammo reloaded while the other nine units pass by. We continue rotating every hour like that throughout the day and night. Two or three times a day, when we receive heavy resistance, we may stop everyone. When that happens, there's extra fighter plane and helicopter gun support. They have lost several vehicles to roadside bombs. It's always the lead unit that takes the heaviest gunfire from individuals, often groups of five to twenty people with their hunting rifles and other types of arms. In many places there are a lot of dead and wounded left along the highways."

"What else is happening that you can tell us about?"

"Well, when the highway goes through or near a town, people are grouped along the road. Many of them will have signs that say things like, 'Russians, go home!', 'You will lose!', 'We hate you!' and others I cannot repeat. But on the other hand, I've seen signs and people waving, 'Welcome to America!', 'Peace,' and 'God bless you.' I have not seen or heard of any organized resistance from a state or city government, and we have not seen any military opposition so far. On a few occasions, resistance has come from people in small towns, using rooftops for cover while firing on the army. When the Russian planes come, they destroy everything. Sometimes the resistance will dynamite highway overpasses to stop the army while they move or go around the obstacle. At that point there is usually a big ambush ending with a lot of people dead. I could tell from what I have seen, most of the dead were Americans. I've seen strange things like people trying to join up with the Russians, people coming out to the highway to sell food and things to the Russian soldiers. Sometimes I see people waving Russian flags along the road. Sometimes young women will be waving and smiling at the soldiers."

A Russian voice broke in from behind Morales. "We are moving!"

Morales said, "I have to go. I'll check back when I can."

Out West, Brad and his family, like many others, struggled to get by one day at a time. With the uncertainty of what was going to happen, plans could only be made for each day as it came. The main highways going east out of Seattle, San Francisco, and Los Angeles were completely filled with Chinese troops, armed vehicles, and troop-transport vehicles. Near each town or city, many women with young children gathered near the highway intersections and waved Chinese flags. Chinese and United States military aircraft constantly came and went in all directions. The United States military set up eight training bases throughout the western states to train men and women who enlisted by the thousands.

Brad's company had a contract to build buildings, housing, and barracks on one of the new bases nearby. Carol and Bailey both worked together at the local hospital, where many wounded from the first attack were still being treated.

All western states set curfews and lights-out from sunset to sunrise. Most church buildings were full on Sunday. On many nights throughout the week, after work and before lights-out, people came by as groups or individuals to pray. Gang fighting and rioting still occurred at night in the largest cities, with the police arresting people, but not shooting them like in the East.

On the 10th day of war, Chinese ships began to make port in Seattle and San Francisco, carrying more troops and arms. The Chinese were well-stocked with the latest and best military equipment the United States had given them to fight the Russians. High-level talks began between the United States and Chinese high commands to prepare for their joint-army attack on the Russian armies making their way west.

The exact location of the U.S. government was not publicly announced, but most people knew they were in Las Vegas where there were hotels for government employees, their families, and other staff. The Vegas Convention Center was converted into offices for the President and Vice-President, Congress, Senate, and Supreme Court. Another large building was occupied by the War Department. Other smaller buildings were taken over for government agencies and departments. Vegas had no tourists now. The whole city was in lockdown. No one came or went except through high security. It was public knowledge that most of the Hollywood movie stars had left for Canada, New Zealand, and Australia. The U.S. government estimated that more than one-third of the U.S. general population had fled across the Canadian and Mexican borders, with most going south. Thousands of different boats could be seen crossing the Gulf of Mexico from the United States.

Back at Eagle News in New York City on day ten at 7:10 a.m. EST, the Morning Eagles were in the middle of their program with Steve Harmon reporting. "The baseball commissioner has announced that all spring training has been suspended, and baseball season is cancelled until further notice."

A news alert banner flashed on the screen. Randy Wade appeared and began to speak. "It is reported by a number of internet bloggers that over the last two nights there were six different internet bloggers across the country whose families have been killed in their homes and their homes burned. Two of them were in the west. The bloggers also said there were several other bloggers who spoke disrespectfully of the Russians, and also wrote information they had been warned not to write."

Harmon spoke up. "We know the social media companies were warned, like the TV and newspaper people, that if they didn't follow the same rules, they would be subject to being put out of business. They have slowed down all of the posted entries, and Twitter shut down completely because they couldn't be monitored. Also, it seems that all of the power grids east of the Rocky Mountains have been hacked into and are being controlled by someone else. We could lose all power if someone wanted it so."

Wade said, "With the way things are, all of us must be careful what we say publicly."

Judy Best came on next. "We have a special guest this morning." The camera backed up to show Judy and a female guest seated opposite each other at a small table. Judy said, "With us this morning is historian and author Lacie McConnell." She turned to Lacie. "Welcome. We are glad you could be here this morning."

"Thanks for having me," Lacie replied.

"Is it true that you're already working on a book about the war?"

"Yes, I am. From a historical point of view, it's important that I start now to keep all my facts as accurate as possible."

"You also wrote an article in the *Wall Street Journal* entitled 'The Last Invasion.' Can you tell us about that article?"

"Yes, Judy," she said. "'The Last Invasion' in the United States happened in 1812 when, like this invasion, the British pulled off a sneak attack on Washington, D.C. Their ships arrived in the Chesapeake Bay unloading troops who marched into Washington, D.C. There was some resistance along the way, but there was none in the city. Everyone had fled before the invaders arrived. On the first day they began burning down the city; first the Capitol building, then the White House, followed by many other lesser buildings. They were very disrespectful to the office of the President and his home. That first night they made their plans to burn the rest of the city the next day." Lacie turned to face the camera. "However, later that evening and on through the night, there came one of the most powerful storms ever seen in those parts. The rains were so heavy it put out the fires. The winds were so fierce, they crushed the British army down. That night more British were killed and wounded from the storm than from the militia the day before. One British soldier wrote, 'It was as if God, Himself, beat us down.' The next day, devastated and disorganized, they returned to their ships and went north to Baltimore where they lost the battle for the Americas and retreated."

"That's an amazing story of our history, Lacie," Judy said.

"But God has not come to our aid like that yet."

"Maybe He will," Lacie replied. "Then again, maybe we do not deserve His help. Only time will tell." Lacie went on to say, "War is terrible, but there have always been wars. They go on all over the world all the time. Less than one hundred years ago, the world lost thirty-two million people in World Wars I and II."

"I wish you luck on your new book," Judy said.

"Thanks," Lacie said.

On the afternoon of the eleventh day at 3:45 p.m. EST, Nancy Coleman and Wayne Cannon were in the middle of their late afternoon broadcast, switching from story to story. Nancy finished by saying, "After ten days of rioting and looting, there is less now than there was, but in some places people have turned to breaking into houses and stealing from the homes that people have abandoned. Most cities report looters are still being shot, as well as those who attack police. There are also fewer reports of suicide."

A special report banner with "Our Nation Under Siege" flashed on the screen, followed by Wayne Cannon. "We have news from our reporter David Wade, somewhere near the Russian army."

David appeared on one of the monitors, and Cannon asked, "David, can you tell us where you are?"

"Yes, Wayne. I can tell you that we came up by car from D.C. to the south side of one of the Russian armies moving west on US-70. At Indianapolis they turned northwest on 74. It is common knowledge now that the lead units have just turned west on 80 at Grand Rapids. We are moving west on highway 40 which is parallel to US-70. We cannot keep up with the army because the traffic on the side roads is moving so slow. In towns close to the interstate, local people have blocked roads going

in and out, checked us for ID, and asked us what we were doing there. They also checked the vehicle for any weapons. They are trying to stop anyone from attacking the army from their town because they know that retaliation is swift and devastating." Wade paused. "We are now stopped in London, Ohio, to rest and get this report to you at Eagle. We have uploaded a lot of video back to you in New York."

"Yes, David, we have been getting it," Cannon said. "They have put it together but were waiting for you to call and walk us through it."

"Have you seen it?" David asked.

"Yes, I've seen it," Cannon said. "It's a very disturbing and graphic video."

"We should warn the viewers."

Cannon turned and spoke directly to the viewing audience. "I do not believe this video content is suitable for children, or for those who cannot bear to look on the dead." He paused and turned slightly. "David."

"In the beginning, even before the invasion, the Russians said that they would try to not harm the U.S. citizen population, and they would treat the military with due respect. From all we have been able to see, that has been the case. But civilians who attack them, or try to stop them in some way, are given no mercy. We have spoken to people in almost every town we've been through, and they all have stories to tell about what has happened. There seems to be groups of the army that travel on both sides. The Russians call them death squads. Some of the people call them torture squads." David hesitated as if he didn't want to continue. After a few seconds he spoke again. "When a person, or persons, attack the army and are killed, wounded or captured, the death squads come along and strip them naked and tie their legs together at their ankles. Then they drive spikes into telephone poles and trees along the road and hang them upside-down with their faces looking out. Many times, there are four people on a telephone pole. They can be heard crying out until they're dead--men and women, young and old who tried to attack the Russian military." David stopped a moment. His body shuddered visibly. "Throughout the day the buzzards will land on them and eat their faces and other parts of their bodies. Now more and more people are risking their own lives to sneak out in the middle of the night and take them down. Especially the ones that may still be alive."

As David described the process, viewers could see for themselves miles and miles of telephone poles, an indescribably horrific sight.

"This must not only be terrible to see, but to hear live along the road," Cannon said softly.

"Yes," David said. "It's even worse seeing it live. Its purpose of course is to put fear in the hearts of the people, much like how the Roman armies would crucify thousands of people along the roads as travelers passed by. People will think about what they are seeing and it will certainly keep many of them from coming after the army."

"David, why are they stripping them?"

"We're not sure, Wayne. Some who spoke with us said the Russians burn all their clothes, personal possessions, even cell phones at the end of the day. I believe it's to humiliate them and make identification difficult. Some people who recover the bodies will take pictures for future identification and then burn the bodies."

"David, what else can you tell us about what's going on out there?"

"Well, no one else can travel on the three interstate highways the Russians are using. You can cross over or under, but they're moving a lot of troops and supplies out west. Empty trucks are returning east. They're building an outpost around the highway about every 50 miles, always between towns or cities. At these places there are hospitals, first aid, and fuel. Every other post has gas tanks buried in the ground, receiving fuel from Exxon and BP. Both companies agreed to sell them fuel after the Russians explained that if they did not, they would not have a refinery standing anywhere in the world." David paused. "We crossed over the highway twice; once going north, and once going back south the next day. All overpasses are well barricaded and Russian soldiers check our vehicles for weapons and bombs then send us on our way with a warning, 'Do not stop on the overpass or bridge.' We made a video each time from the car as you can see. There are three lanes moving west and only one going east. The army stretches out as far as you can see. Hundreds of Humvee-type vehicles with trailers attached, are loaded with a missile-type system on the trailers that could be fired at will, moving or stopped. Surprisingly, there are no tanks or heavy vehicles. All are rubber-tired for fast moving on our interstates. Slow-moving drones fly above the army looking for problems around them. In some areas people have out signs saying, 'Welcome!' 'Peace!' and a few people waving small Russian flags. We had some reports from people that Russian soldiers would come into town and buy food from the hamburger places. They were well armed and polite. They paid for their food and left." David broke off from his report and said, "We have to go now. We just heard there was an attack about 60 miles ahead. We will try to check back in tomorrow with an update."

Cannon ended the interview with, "David, from your dad and all of us, be very careful out there."

"Yes, Wayne, we will," David assured him.

Whoever will not observe the law of your God and the law of the king, let judgment be executed speedily on him, whether it be death, or banishment, or confiscation of goods, or imprisonment.
-Ezra 7:26

CHAPTER 8

THE SURPRISE ANNOUNCEMENT

It was 10 a.m. Mountain Standard Time in Las Vegas, Nevada. The city had been long deserted of most of its civilian population. Many of the hotels were filled with government employees and family. Security coming in and going out of the city was extremely high. All roads were blocked by Chinese and U.S. military. Today, few were allowed in the city around the convention area and down the entire Las Vegas Strip.

For the past four days the U.S. and Chinese military strategists had been meeting in what they called the War Department building, hammering out plans for the upcoming attack. It was now 2 p.m. The President, Vice President, all congressmen, and the Supreme Court had been meeting in the war room since 10 a.m. They were there for two things: to understand what the generals' attack plans were, and to draft a declaration of war to be voted on and approved by every senator and representative of the United States. No one was allowed in or out of the building.

Adjacent to the war room was another large room where people were making finishing touches for the night's announcement from the President. There was a long table on a raised platform. A speaker's podium stood in the middle, with the President's Seal attached to it.

Centered on the floor level in front of the table were a group of chairs adequate to seat the Supreme Court. To the right and left of those chairs were enough seats for the Senate and the House of Representatives. Behind those groups were

chairs for two hundred people who were there to observe this occasion. Behind these stood an Eagle News camera with a table and two chairs. There were also six security cameras located around the room to catch any actions that might cause problems. Outside there were Eagle satellite trucks filled with news and technical staff making ready for the President's address to the nation at 8 p.m. EST and 6 p.m. local time. The tension was thick enough to cut with a knife.

The government and military were on high alert, extremely concerned about reports the past two days from night-time fishermen spotting black Russian subs a few miles off the West Coast. Reports of the subs came in from Seattle to Los Angeles. All U.S. communications and spy satellites had been rendered inoperable by the Russians, making verification of the subs impossible.

Henry King, Eagle reporter and commentator, entered the building to prepare for the evening broadcast. He was accompanied by the popular Eagle Talk Show host, Joseph Warren, who had been in Los Angeles since the invasion started. Unable to get back to New York, he had been working for Eagle from L.A. The two men went over what was scheduled to happen in the next few hours. They reviewed stories they would be talking about leading up to the speech.

Two hours before the President was to speak, security around the buildings was tight. One TV crewman was heard to say, "There are more Chinese guarding this building than there are in China."

Thirty large buses had parked in front of the building filled with members of congressional families from nearby hotels. Joseph Warren asked Henry King, "What do you make of the buses and families?"

King said, "All of this was planned ahead. When the declaration of war is announced, the President, Vice President, the congressional members, and the Supreme Court members will be rushed out to these buses to be with their families, and taken out of town. I'm sure the Russians know where we all are. This place could be the next target of the war. With the reports of the Russian sub sightings, this will become the most dangerous place on the West Coast. Eagle has three SUVs for us and the crew to also get out of town fast."

At 5:30 p.m. local time, and 7:30 p.m. EST time, the broadcast began. Warren and King talked about what King had seen as a White House correspondent leading up to that moment. They also spoke back and forth with men and women who were seated around a table at the Eagle News studios in New York.

At fifteen minutes before six, the doors between the two buildings were opened. First to come out were the members of the Supreme Court who took their seats. The Senators came and they took their chairs on the right; the House of Representatives took their chairs on the left.

"Everyone is so quiet," King whispered.

Warren responded, "You would be, too. All of their lives are on the line tonight, and from now on. The Russians have said they will leave no one alive from the central government and those men and women know that."

From the right came four U.S. generals and admirals who took the first four chairs at the right side of the table. From the left came four Chinese officers and took the first four seats at the left side of the table. A man in a suit came in and sat next to them. Again from the right came the Secretary of State, the Attorney General, and the Vice President. They took chairs on both sides of the podium. The President entered the room last, and everyone stood until he reached the podium and the doors closed.

The President began. "As the President of the greatest nation in the world, and Commander-in-Chief of our military, I speak with you, the people of America, with full agreement from the members of the Senate and the House who are here before you tonight." A camera showed the members sitting somberly in their chairs. "And with the legal opinion of the Supreme Court, who is also here tonight, and with the advice of our military command from the Army, Navy, and Air Force." Cameras focused on the four high-ranking officers sitting to the right of the president. "We have all agreed and signed a...." He paused, cleared his throat, and began again. "We have all agreed and signed a Declaration of Surrender of the United States government and its military to the government of Russia and to the Republic of China. Both now hold us all captive." Without another word, the large doors reopened. When the President turned and stepped down from the podium, the Vice President, Secretary of State, and Attorney General followed. The silence in the room was broken as all Supreme Court and Congressional members rose and immediately walked to the doors and disappeared into the darkness.

Once they left the room, the doors closed again. General Clark, who was now the chief military officer, slowly rose, straightened his uniform jacket, and went to the podium. "I will spell out the terms of surrender. First, the surrender is unconditional. All U.S. military forces within the continental United States are immediately ordered to lay down their weapons, remove their uniforms, leave their military posts, and return to their homes with only personal belongings.

"All military outside the continental United States are to return to the United States with all equipment and military resources. They are also to disengage and return to their homes. All ships at sea are to return to their home port in the U.S. and leave their ships."

"Any military personnel failing to carry out these commands and the terms of this surrender by the government will be considered in violation of the surrender and will be subject to punishment of death by one of the conquering nations."

Having read the terms and conditions, General Clark turned to leave the podium, followed by the three remaining

U.S. military generals. They, too, walked to the doors, disappeared into the darkness, and the doors closed.

At the Eagle News table in the back of the room, Joseph Warren, in a state of shock slowly turned to Henry King. "Can you believe what just happened?"

King was speechless and could only shake his head in disbelief. Warren turned to the panel in New York. "We understand that our nation has given up and walked away."

Back in New York, Bill Sawyer responded. "We are all here to talk about the war we thought we were going to be in tomorrow. Joseph, we are as stunned as you are. I'm sure all Americans who saw this are asking why we surrendered. The government must know a lot they're not telling us."

"Well, I certainly have a lot of questions. I thought the Chinese were on our side. What happened to them? Did they simply see an opportunity and just took us over? Are they going to go to war against their old enemy, the Russians, here on American soil?"

Randy Wade said, "It reminded me of the Japanese surrender on the Battleship Missouri at the end of World War II, but we did it without a war."

"Wait," Henry King said. "The Chinese general and the man in the black suit are now going to the podium."

Both men stood at the podium and signed several sets of documents. The man in the black suit turned and handed a set of documents to a young Chinese officer standing nearby. The officer took the documents and walked to the Eagle News table. Before he handed the papers of surrender to Henry King, he pointed to the signatures. "Please verify that these are signed by the President and those of the House and Senate."

King took the papers and read each signature. The young officer patiently waited. "Yes, I verify the signatures."

The officer said, "Keep those in a safe place for the

people of this country." Then he turned to walk away.

Warren quickly asked, "Where are the men and women of the government?"

The young officer turned back and replied, "They and their families are together in a place of safety." The young man added, "Each state government is now receiving documents indicating to which country that state will belong, and the laws under which they are free to govern their state and its people." He turned and walked away and the remaining people in the room followed him out.

Warren and King stood up. "There's no more for us to report from here. We will make our way back to New York."

In the Eagle News control room Mr. Blackburn, other executives, and program producers sat in stunned silence. Mr. Blackburn finally gathered his thoughts and spoke. "We have just witnessed an unimaginable event of monumental importance. At this moment I am not able to make further comment."

From his usual place, Zachar observed the surrender and the reaction of those in the room. He rose purposefully and walked across the room to Mr. Blackburn. Blackburn rose and met him eye to eye.

Zachar said, "My time is done. I, and my people, will be gone from your premises before midnight. Eagle is now, and always was, your business. I was only here to keep you safe. Remember, I chose you because you were the most true and reliable of all the media outlets. I hope you will remain so in the future. But I must give you warning as I leave. Do not lie or be disrespectful towards the ones who are appointed over you, whether it be a new military government or your own state government, because we are going to remain here to keep you safe from your enemies."

"What enemies are you going to protect us from?" Blackburn questioned.

Zachar smiled, holding eye contact with Blackburn. "From your greatest enemy: yourselves." Zachar gave a casual salute and walked out of the room.

In Oregon, Brad and his family met with other members at the church building to pray for the leaders of the nation, the military, and to hear the President's message. Life would never be the same. The President's message changed everything.

Afterwards, they discussed what God would have them do, and again prayed for the Lord's church in every place, and for peace in the land with the new government they would now be under. Tomorrow was Sunday. They would return to worship the true and living God, and to honor His Son, Jesus the Christ as King and High Priest, knowing when Monday came, they would begin their lives together under a new government. And they would continue to work, feed their families, and live day by day.

Changes that affected every person in America came swiftly. The country was divided east of the Rocky Mountains. Each state was given new laws and requirements from the new military government, with only 30 days to write and legally pass a new state constitution, pledging allegiance to their new government—either the United States of Russia (to the east) or the United States of China (to the west). Any state not having a completed and approved constitution would have military rule and no elected governor.

Each state was allowed the power to elect its own leaders and govern itself under the new laws they had to adopt, but had only 60 days to pass and implement all the new laws and regulations. All new laws would be upheld by all judges currently sitting in court.

For minor crimes of two years or less, sentences would be served in city or county jails. Sentences of two to five years would be served in state jails. Anyone with more than five years would be turned over to the military to serve their time in China or Russia.

Crimes calling for the death penalty would be carried out by military firing squads. Those crimes would include murder against anyone, attack of any kind toward a government or military official, disrespect toward any government or any military personnel, assault with attempt to kill, armed robbery, kidnapping, any government official or judge misusing their office, anyone found guilty of lying in a court of law, anyone bringing false evidence or false claims in a court of law, anyone found guilty of paying or accepting a bribe, and sex crimes against children. Punishment for these crimes would be carried out no later than 30 days from the day of conviction.

Each state also had 6 months to issue a credit-card style ID to every person residing in that state. The card would hold a micro-chip provided by the new military government, with information for the state's use. All ID cards were to be in the person's possession at all times. If detained for any reason by the government, police, or military, the card must be shown. If a card was lost or misplaced, the person would receive one year in jail for the first offense, two years for the second offense, and deportation for the third offense. Anyone without a card, or found with a counterfeit card, would be deported immediately.

The ID card, when inserted into an ID tablet, would show a picture of the person, a picture of any birthmarks or tattoos, fingerprints, the DNA of the card-holder, and all general information about the person: place of birth, age, address, education, family information—spouse and children, religion, occupation and position, driver's license, and medical history.

The Russian and Chinese armies would provide military protection for each state, and each state must pay for the protection as well as make payments to pay off the invasion costs. Each state would tax the people by sales tax and businesses by income tax.

Within 60 days the Chinese and Russian armies had locked down the northern and southern U.S. borders. Signs were posted warning that anyone crossing would be executed. Cameras covered all border areas. Drones flew in the sky, and landmines were placed as far away as one mile from each border.

All entry into the United States had to go through the Chinese or Russian embassies, where a visa was required for a visit. Citizenship could not be applied for until one year after the invasion. Any citizen who had previously left the country would be required to wait five years before reapplying for new citizenship.

All air travel in the U.S. would be reinstated in 30 days, but there would be no international air travel in or out of the U.S. for one year. Both Chinese and Russians would allow immigration into the U.S. from their countries.

The United States of Russia was economically bankrupt. Unemployment was high, but the law provided for former military to have priority for hiring. The United States of China was better off but still not good. All old government lands were given to the state where they were located. The Chinese stock market in San Francisco and the Russian stock market in New York City tried to open four times but had to immediately close each time. Large banks had difficulty staying open. Small banks simply closed their doors.

The Chinese and Russian governments removed all U.S. gold and silver reserves, divided them up, and took them to their own countries. All U.S. dollars would now be backed by the conquering nation's currency.

Depression was worldwide. There was no longer money from the United States to help the poor countries. China itself was hard hit financially because it was unable to produce items to export back to the United States.

Government welfare, as previously known, was gone. Each state was required to have a job for unemployed residents. Those who were unwilling to work would have nothing to eat. Those too young, too old, or mentally or physically unable to work, had to seek food and shelter from churches and private organizations. Health insurance companies and retirement funds

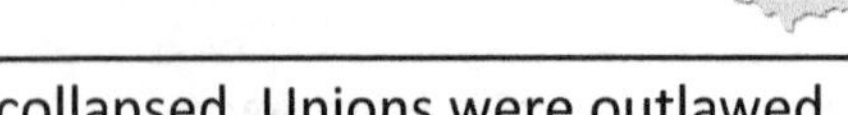

collapsed. Unions were outlawed.

People lost faith and hope in the government. They also lost faith and hope in their possessions. On Sundays, nearly every church building was filled. People were returning to God for that same faith and hope, knowing He was the only One who could help them.

The new military government established offices in each state's capital to provide a liaison between the state and military governments. English was the only recognized national language. All persons coming to the United States, even from China and Russia, would be required to learn English. Each state would be responsible for its school and hospital systems, and also be responsible for the medical needs of all military personnel. To keep peace within each state and for help during natural disasters, each state would keep its National Guard and state police.

Over the next six months unrest continued. There were clashes between individuals or small groups against the conquering military. Many lives were lost on each side. No mercy was shown to those who were against the conquering nations. All wounded or captured continued to be stripped and hung upside-down to die by the Russians. The Chinese did the same, except they would lay the bodies along the road afterward for all to see. None were left alive. The government buildings and monuments in Washington, D.C. were fenced off and made off-limits to everyone. The remaining part of Washington, D.C. was given to the state of Virginia.

The defeat of America had worldwide repercussions, sending most of the world into a depression. Three countries in Europe had their governments taken over by Muslims, resulting in the collapse of the Euro. England's economy was hit the hardest and went financially bankrupt. North Korea invaded South Korea. Now that America could not help, many tyrannical dictators took over their neighboring countries. It was estimated that over 100,000 died each day worldwide.

CHAPTER 9

THE MEETING

Sunday, the 15th day of the seventh month after the war, Brad and his family were a half hour into their worship service when three men and a woman entered the auditorium. They were all dressed in casual black. Two of the men and the woman stood just inside the door of the auditorium. The other man approached the podium and asked to deliver some emergency information.

The preacher stepped aside and quietly asked, "What is the emergency?"

The man in black ignored the question but turned to the audience and said, "For your safety, each one of you must immediately place any weapons and cell phones on the floor in front of you. Then stand and make your way into the aisles."

The people were not certain what was going on, but knew they must follow the instructions. When they stood and turned around, six armed Chinese soldiers entered the building. One soldier began making a minimal search of each adult in the line at the back of the auditorium. Two of the men in black asked for ID cards, placing each one in their tablet reader to verify a picture of the person to make certain they had the right card. The other man in black asked each person, "Are you and your family Christians?" If the answer was no, they were told to leave and to get their ID card updated immediately.

All who said they were Christians were taken out of the

building and put on one of two large buses that were in the parking lot. All were afraid. Several repeatedly asked, "What's going on?" but received no answer.

When both buses were full, one soldier and one of those dressed in black got on the bus and the bus left. Those sitting near the front of the bus again asked the one in black where they were going, but still received no answer. As the bus pulled away, one of the soldiers remaining made certain all the cars in the parking lot were locked.

Although the bus windows were darkly tinted, Brad saw the sign when the bus turned onto I-5 heading north toward Portland. There was nothing to do at that point but to pray God would protect them from whatever might happen.

Later in the afternoon, Brad recognized that they were in Portland, waiting in a line of buses in front of a large sports-arena-type building. Their bus doors opened and the man in black said, "Go immediately into the building." Without speaking, Brad, his family, and everyone else stepped off the bus and merged with the line of other people going in. Armed soldiers lined the walkway on both sides.
Inside the building there appeared to be several thousand people already present. Most were in family groups and with those who had ridden the same bus. Well-armed Chinese soldiers stood in front of all exit doors.

A voice announced over the speaker system in English, "All people who are of the Jewish religion, line up at door A." The doors opened. As people passed through, their cards with their information were not only examined, but also copied. They seemed to be making a list of all who entered door A.

Thirty minutes later the voice again announced, "All persons who are of the Muslim religion come to door C." They were processed as those at door A. Then followed the announcement for any Catholic to go through door B. Then all Protestants were called to doors D and E.

The last call was for Christians to assemble at door F. Brad and his family moved to the area with the remaining people. Again, Chinese dressed in casual black stood ready to process them in the same manner as the other lines, requiring each person's ID card. Here, too, people were identified, and copies were made, as if a list was being compiled.

Brad asked, "What is going on?" No response. "Why are you holding us? We are United States citizens and we have done nothing wrong." Again, there was no response. When Brad and his family were next in line, he stepped in front of his family and spoke in a stronger voice to the man in black, who seemed to be in charge. "I demand as a United States citizen that you tell me why we are being detained like this and what is going on!" No answer. "Why are we being held against our will?" The man in charge appeared to pay no attention to Brad as he looked over the people in the line.

A Chinese soldier stepped between Brad and the man in black. "Get back in line," he spoke firmly, then added, "Just do what you're told and answer the question."

Brad stared at the man a moment then asked, "What question?" No one answered.

A few moments later the man in black spoke again in a quieter voice, "Move your family forward 20 feet," he said and pointed to where a Chinese man and woman stood dressed in the same casual black.

"Are you a Christian?" the man asked.

Brad and his family then realized that for some reason the Chinese were looking for Christians. Each answered, "Yes."

The woman said, "If you tell us that you are not a Christian, you will be free to go."

Brad and Carol looked at each other, then at Kasey and

Bailey. They understood that all they would have to do was lie, deny being a Christian, and they would be free to go. But they also knew that was not something they could do. Each one answered without hesitation, "I am a Christian."

An interrogator stood in front of each one of them and asked, "Is being a Christian so important that you would give your life?"

Brad, Carol, Kasey, and Bailey then understood the possible cost for what they believed. Again, although their hearts were pounding, each one repeated without hesitation, "I am a Christian." They were handed a white sticker with a red "C" written on it, and instructions to place it on their clothing.

When the stickers were in place, the Chinese man in black waved his arm and said, "Go into the next room. Take the exit door marked 'C.'"

A soldier directed Brad and his family to the door marked "C." Down the way on another wall was a similar door marked NC. Going through Door C they found themselves outside, where buses lined the road around the building as far as could be seen. They were loaded onto a bus and when it was full, it departed heading southeast out of Portland.

On the bus, most people prayed, asking the Lord to help them. Others spoke quietly to each other about what might be happening to them. Some near the front of the bus asked the soldiers again where they were going. One of the passengers spoke of Hitler and the death camps of World War II. Everyone was afraid, not knowing what would be their fate.

It was almost dark as the bus pulled into a place that looked familiar to Brad. It was the new military training base that his company had been contracted to build, only finished two months ago for the new military government. There were lights on in some of the buildings. When the bus pulled through the large gates and passed a large brightly-lit building, Brad could see people looking out of the windows.

The bus stopped in front of another well-lit area and they were told to get off. As they departed the bus, a number of heavily armed Chinese soldiers could be seen at the edge of the area. When the buses pulled away, the people found themselves inside a compound surrounded by a high fence with lights and cameras. A group of Chinese soldiers suddenly appeared from the area behind them.

With the soldiers was one of the Chinese men dressed in black. He stood in front of them and said with a smile, "Welcome to your new home. I am Ming Lee, the camp commander." His English was blanketed with a heavy Chinese accent. He continued, "My office and quarters are over there." He gestured toward a nice building just outside and to the right of the big gate. He went on to say, "You can send a representative to see me if you have any needs. Do not ask me why you are here, when you will leave, or if you can make calls. These types of questions I cannot and will not answer." He looked at various people in the group, then added, "There are some here now and there will be many more to come. You must get together with the others and select your leaders to govern and organize yourselves to live here for some unknown time. Food will be delivered to you each day. You will prepare and feed yourselves. Please remember that there is a shortage of food throughout the land. Use wisely what we give you. We will provide some seeds for a garden and animals from the local farmers. If there are any medical emergencies, there are doctors nearby who can come and care for you. There is also a supply office that will be open during the day. One of my assistants will supply the best we can to provide for your needs."

The officer paused a few seconds and looked toward the armed soldiers who stood a few feet away from the group. "Let me warn you," he spoke again. "Stay away from the fences and do not talk with the soldiers who are guarding you. Only a few understand or speak English. All guards will be on the outside of the fence unless they are here with me. These

soldiers only know that they must keep you here and if anyone is found outside the fence, they are to shoot without warning. Remember that you are in a dangerous place and these are dangerous times. If you break the rules, I cannot help you. Be very careful." Then the commander motioned to the soldiers and they went out the way they came in.

Brad and his family, with others from the buses, walked to the nearest brightly-lit building. The entry hall ran front to back. The other hall ran right to left the length of the building with rooms on both sides. The people walked down the hall in both directions, opening doors and claiming rooms for their families. Sparsely furnished rooms held four cots with linens and a pillow for each, and a small sink in the corner to the left of the door. A shelf held four towels and washcloths. A small, wood-burning stove stood in the middle of the room. A window with a plain fabric curtain faced the compound yard.

"At least it's clean," Carol said softly.

Kasey grabbed one of the cots and walked across the room with it. "I claim this corner," he said, sounding almost jovial.

Bailey frowned, picked up the end of another cot, and dragged it to the opposite corner in silence.

"Well," Brad said, looking around the room as if trying to make a decision. "Let's go there." He pointed to the corner opposite the sink.

"Great choice," Carol agreed and pulled her cot next to Brad's.

Bailey sat down on her cot and stared at the pillow. She rubbed her hands back and forth across it a couple of times, then laid down and turned over facing the wall, hugging the pillow to her. Brad and Carol watched with concern but said nothing.

Brad looked at Kasey. "Let's go check on our neighbors and see if they need help. Then we'll see what can be done for food."

"Great idea, Dad," Kasey said and followed Brad out the door.

Carol watched Bailey and offered her own silent prayer for their protection and strength to face the unknown future. She remained in prayerful thoughts a little longer then went to Bailey's cot. "Bailey, are you awake?"

Bailey sat up and grabbed her mother in a hug that only a mother could give a child seeking comfort. "Oh, Mom. I'm so scared! Why is God doing this to us?" she asked, tears rolling down her cheeks.

"Oh Bailey, Honey, God isn't doing anything to us. People we don't even know have made decisions on their own that will affect us for a long, long time. We're victims of what they are doing. God will protect us and give us His providential care. I know this room may not be your idea of provision, but it's clean and it's indoors. I'm thankful we're not out in the open and sleeping on the ground."

"Mom, you're always so positive. How do you do it?"

"You learn to trust God, and hope for Heaven. Keep your faith strong, Bailey. Always look for the good in any situation. And take life one day at a time." She stroked her daughter's cheek.

Bailey leaned against Carol and sniffled. "I wish I could be like you."

"It comes with maturity. Trust God in the hard times to give you strength and help you through them. He won't let you

down."

Bailey thought about it. "I'll try, Mom. I really will."

"I know you will, Honey." Bailey sat up and Carol brushed her hair back. "Okay now. Dry your eyes and let's go find Dad and Kasey. Others may need our help."

Over the next few weeks buses arrived almost daily, but more so on Sundays and Mondays, until the camp was full. Brad and the camp leaders tried to visit with the new people to learn what was going on outside. A couple of men who understood Chinese had heard it was for population reorganization and there was nothing to fear, but they weren't sure.

From time to time some were taken away in buses and never returned. Some resisted and were killed. Anyone who was a Jew or Muslim was also taken away, as were some Christians, homosexuals, and people who could not prove their citizenship. If anyone was stopped for any reason, the main question asked was, "What is your religion?" If the person was a registered atheist, had no religion, or did not claim to believe in God or Jesus, the Chinese seemed to not care about that person, and let them go.

When Brad heard that, he remembered that most Chinese are taught there is no God, so they would be considered atheists. It was taught in their schools. "Maybe the new government wants us to be a nation of atheists," Brad mumbled to himself.

Two weeks later on Monday night a black SUV pulled up at the camp commander's office just outside the compound gate. One of the assistants to the camp commander and two soldiers came into the compound looking for Brad. When they found him, they asked for his ID card, checked his information, and asked a couple of questions to make sure that he was in fact Brad Wilson. "Are any of your family members here with you?"

one of the assistants asked.

"Yes, my wife, son, and daughter."

"Get them and your belongings. You are leaving here now."

"Where are we going?" Brad asked.

The assistant replied, "You will find out. Get them. You must go now."

Brad hurried back to his family's living quarters. "Pack our things in some plastic bags. We're leaving here now."

The three of them spoke at once. "What?" "Why?" "Where?"

Brad threw his hands up in front of him, palms out, and shook his head in a silent no. "We don't have time to talk. Just do it quickly. There's a car waiting outside for us right now. There's no time to explain."

Within minutes, the four of them were in the SUV with one of those in black driving and an armed Chinese soldier in the front passenger seat. After midnight, they arrived at the Portland train station where they were put in a locked compartment on a train headed south. The train carried mostly Chinese soldiers, but there were some cars filled with people under guard.

The train arrived in San Francisco mid-afternoon the next day. Then, along with some others from the train, they were taken by bus to an island in the middle of San Francisco bay, a long-time American Naval base known as Treasure Island. It was now a heavily armed Chinese military base.

Brad and his family were tired from their trip but knew they had to keep going. They were taken into a large building and placed in a holding cell. From there, people could be seen and heard in what Brad thought might be interrogation rooms. Most of the people walking in the halls were dressed in black.

There were Chinese soldiers, but they wore uniforms that Brad had not seen before—tan uniforms with a black right sleeve. A few times they heard yelling from various rooms and once, from outside the building, they heard what sounded like gunshots. Later, from a room down the hall they heard what sounded like a single pistol shot. There were soldiers moving people from place to place at gunpoint. Brad and his family sat on the floor, held hands, and prayed.

Half an hour later a woman in black came to their cell with two armed soldiers dressed in the tan uniforms with the black sleeves. The woman asked for Brad's ID card to once again confirm who he was. Then one of the soldiers put Brad's arms behind his back and secured him.

"Where are you taking my husband?" Carol demanded.

Kasey stepped beside his dad. "Take me. I'm younger. Leave my dad here."

As usual, no answers were given. The holding-cell door was closed and locked behind them as the woman in black, the two soldiers, and Brad went around the corner and out of sight.

Brad was taken out of that building and across to another building even more heavily guarded. Again at the door, there were four soldiers. They not only checked Brad's ID but the ID of the woman in black. Entering the building, Brad and the woman in black were accompanied by one of the soldiers who had been at the entrance to the building. They walked down a wide hallway to a set of double doors on the left, also guarded with two more soldiers standing guard in the hall, one on each side of the doors. The woman in black stepped through one of the double doors, leaving Brad with the two soldiers standing guard. Less than two minutes later the door opened again. A soldier with a black sleeve came out of the room and removed the restraints from Brad's arms, then turned and went down the hall. A minute later, the woman in black opened the door and motioned Brad to enter. The two soldiers followed him into the room.

A large desk stood in the middle of the room with a massive map of the United States on the wall behind it. A dark line ran from north to south along the east side of the Rocky Mountains. On the east side was marked "U.S. of Russia" and on the west side "U.S. of China." Different colored pins identified places on the Chinese side of the map. Two people dressed in black stood talking as they looked at a tablet. Across the room there were two more black-sleeved soldiers talking with another person who was also dressed in black.

Brad looked down at the desk where he stood. There was another ID tablet laying face-up with his picture on it. The hair on the back of his neck stood up. His heart began to pound. *I wish I could have hugged my family good-bye.*

As Brad stood in front of the desk with a soldier on each side of him, he again looked back to the large map on the wall behind the desk. There were colored pins: red, black, green, and white. He could tell that a white pin was at the camp he and his family had just left. As Brad studied the map, he could see three white pins located on the west side of the Rocky Mountains and four white pins just to the east of the Rocky Mountains.

Suddenly from behind him someone entered the room and spoke a sentence or two in Chinese. At that point, everyone else in the room left. The man made his way around Brad to the other side of the desk. He was well-dressed in a black uniform with three gold stars on each shoulder and gold braid around the cuff of his right sleeve. He wore a beret-styled cap with three gold stars on the front. He opened a desk drawer, removed a book and placed it on the desk in front of Brad.

Brad looked down and immediately recognized it as a well-worn Bible. He blinked, looked again, and saw his own name embossed in the lower right hand corner of the leather. When he looked up at the man across the desk from him, he saw a very happy Chinese man with a big smile on his face who said, "Brad, it is me, John. You cared for me in your house almost three years ago in a winter storm."

A feeling of immense relief passed through Brad's body

that was so intense, he almost fell over. He studied the face of the man, glanced down at the Bible, and back up at the man facing him. Yes, he could see it was John, the man they had rescued in the snow storm, but who now wore a pencil mustache and a more mature appearance. Brad didn't know what to say. John came around the desk where Brad stood and the two men embraced.

"I have been waiting for your name to show up in our system for a long time," John said. "As soon as I found you, I sent for you." John motioned for Brad to sit down in one of the chairs in front of the desk. When they were seated, John reached over and picked up the Bible. "I have much to tell you about all that has happened since the last time we saw each other." He paused, still smiling at Brad. "I remembered all the things you had told me about the special people of God and their Lord and Savior, His Son, and how I could know all about them in this Bible you gave me." John held up the book. "I began to read it and the more I read, the more I wanted to read. I could not put it down. I read it over three times as I remembered that you told me that it was the Word of God. I also remembered that you were sure there were some of these special Christians, who were faithful ones, in China. I began to look for them, and sure enough, when I understood what I was looking for, I found them. I secretly began to meet with two different groups in two different places. They were what you said: people who loved God and their Lord and Savior, who put Them first in their lives, and would do all that they could to be what Jesus expected of them. In only a few weeks I knew I had to be one of these faithful children of God. A few weeks later, they secretly took me to a place where there was enough water and I was baptized for the remission of my sins. I faithfully worshipped with them until I left China. I repented of my sins, married Mary, taught her, and she, too, became a Christian. I then understood that maybe God had placed me in a very special position and I now had to do something to help the Lord's people in America. I began to realize that because I was one of the planning people, perhaps there was a way that I could make that happen."

Brad was happy to hear of his new brother in Christ, but

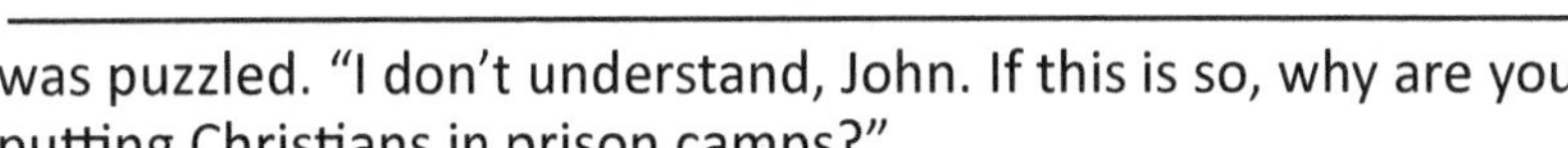

was puzzled. "I don't understand, John. If this is so, why are you putting Christians in prison camps?"

"There is so much I want to tell you but there isn't time. Nor is it wise for you to know too much." John said. "I will tell you soon. Now, I need your help."

"My help?" Brad said, stunned.

"Yes," John replied firmly. "The Lord's people and His Church need your help now."

Brad frowned as he looked at John. "Now I really don't understand."

John rose from his chair and said, "Come over here." The two men moved to stand in front of the big map behind John's desk. John pointed to the white pin marking the holding camp where Brad and his family had been. Then he pointed to all of the other white pins and said, "Like where you were, there are six more."

Brad couldn't understand how he could help. John said, "I need you to go immediately to each of these camps and meet with camp leaders and all the men who serve as elders of the Lord's Church. You need to assure them that they are not in any danger and there is no plan to harm them. They will be released soon. I cannot say now when that will be. It could be weeks or even months. You need to do this so that there will not be fear in their hearts as there is now. But," he paused, looked a moment at Brad, then continued, "You also need to warn them not to tell this to anyone outside the camp."

Brad looked at John, then the map, then back at John. "I will always do what I can for the Lord's Church. How can I do this?"

"I will give you two of my closest assistants to accompany you to each camp, but remember, it is still very dangerous out there. You will have to travel by car." John opened his desk drawer, took out a metal box and placed his hand on it which identified him and it opened. He took out a new ID card. "Give me your old ID card. I have prepared this new card for you. This new card, when scanned for your picture, will appear with Chinese lettering which will make the person reading your card unable to see past your picture except for the message indicating that you have the highest authority and can go almost any place without difficulty. No one will dare question you or keep you from anywhere you wish to go. Remember, be humble with this power."

While John inserted the new ID card into the reader to assure it was as he said, Brad asked, "What about my family? They are here somewhere in a cell."

"While you were here in my office waiting for me, I met with them and assured them that all is well. They were taken to my home where Mary and our child are. We will go there so you can see them and tell them you are going away. They can stay with Mary and I until you return."

Remind them to be subject to rulers and authorities, to obey, to be ready for every good work, to speak evil of no one, to be peaceable, gentle, showing all humility to all men. -Titus 3:1-2

Beloved, do not avenge yourselves, but rather give place to wrath; for it is written, "Vengeance is Mine, I will repay," says the Lord. -Romans 12:19

Likewise also these dreamers defile the flesh, reject authority, and speak evil of dignitaries. -Jude 8

CHAPTER 10

THE REQUEST

Brad was gone twelve days traveling and meeting with the leaders of each camp. Upon his return Brad was driven to John and Mary's home.

Mary graciously welcomed Brad. She hugged him and said, "John has also been away for several days. He will not be back for two more days. John thinks it would be good for you and Carol to have a couple of days for yourselves until his return."

Brad and Carol took those two days in San Francisco where they had spent their honeymoon many years ago. On the same day they returned, a man dressed in the familiar black attire came to the door of their quarters. Mary answered the door, spoke briefly in Chinese, then turned to Brad and said, "John is back and wants you to come and meet with him. Go with this man, please." Mary motioned towards the man standing next to her.

The man took him to a location in the hills, a place that appeared to Brad to be highly fortified. They passed through two layers of military security who checked them both, then came to a building that was built into the mountain. A small part of the building stood out from the mountain. There the entrance was guarded with soldiers dressed in regular Chinese tan uniforms. But these Chinese had a gold star on their hats and one gold star on each shoulder. They also had a narrow red band on their right sleeve only. They searched Brad thoroughly in addition to checking his ID card. This was the most secure place he

had ever been. Then Brad and one of the soldiers at the door were allowed to go into the building. As they walked down the wide hallways, Brad could see that it was some type of military headquarters. There were hundreds of military soldiers and a few dressed in the black attire going about their duties.

Brad and the soldier with him stopped in front of a set of double doors with a well-armed soldier on each side. One soldier asked in Chinese for their ID cards and apparently couldn't speak English. He looked at Brad's picture and then at Brad. At that moment the authority message appeared in Chinese. The guard read the message then held out his own tablet to Brad, indicating for Brad to place his hand on it. The guard placed his tablet into a reading device adjacent to one of the doors. Apparently his tablet would send a message into the room beyond the door. Two minutes later, the door opened and there was John who spoke in Chinese to the guards who then moved back to their post. The soldier who had guided Brad to these doors turned and walked away down the hall.

John smiled and said in English, "Come in, Brad."

They entered a large room with close to fifty soldiers working behind monitors and other devices, working on various types of communication. Brad wondered if this was their main headquarters. John led Brad up a set of stairs to an area that overlooked everything in the room. There was also an additional room made of all glass panels. When they entered the room, noise from the larger room ceased. Brad understood that what they said would not be heard by anyone.

John gave Brad a minute to look around then said, "This is the communication headquarters for all of the U.S. of China military command. All military operations come through this place." Across the room on the opposite wall was a large wall map of all of the United States. To the right of that was a portion of the same map that showed only the eastern states. On the left was another map showing the western states.

"For your safety, you must never tell anyone where you have been and what you have seen," John said solemnly.

Brad nodded his head. "Yes, sir."

"I know you have many questions. I told you I would answer them when you return. But remember, you can never tell anyone what I tell you because it could place you and your family in grave danger. Do you understand?"

Brad studied John a moment then replied again, "Yes, sir."

"But first, sit down and tell me how your visits went at the camps."

Brad was glad to report to John. "At every place they were very relieved to get such good news. They were all thankful to the Lord for saving them."

"Good," John said. "Lord willing, their time there will be short." John then changed the subject. "Brad, what is it that you would like to ask me about?"

Maybe I really don't need to know, Brad thought.

John sensed Brad's reluctance and said, "It is alright, my friend. I can answer many of your questions."

Brad looked around at the many activities going on in the war room. He thought to himself, *Just knowing what happened won't change anything. Why not?* Reluctantly Brad said, "America has done a great deal to help your country protect itself from war with the Russians. You acted like you were willing to come to our aid, then you turned against us at the last minute to join with the Russians."

John looked at Brad eye to eye for a few seconds, then said, "It never happened that way."

Brad was silent. He remembered the horrors of war he had witnessed in the media and the fear he had felt firsthand.

John saw the doubt in Brad's eyes. "Let me start from the beginning. Almost 30 years ago, there was a Chinese man in

the military who was given the opportunity to come to America to attend college at UCLA, and one year at West Point. He had traveled around America extensively, and without meaning to, he grew to love America more than his own homeland. By the time he returned to China, he was troubled that America seemed willing to destroy itself from within. Maybe it was out of love for America, or maybe it was something else. But he began to develop a plan that you and I have seen unfolding before our eyes. That would have been the end of it except that he was able to discuss the plan with the president of China. You see, the two men had been close friends from childhood. The two would spend many hours studying the plan. They worked on it for two years, then about fifteen years ago the president gave him permission to see if he could make the plan work."

John continued, "He then went to Russia where he worked at the Chinese Embassy. There he and the Ambassador to China spent two more years looking for the right man who could help him present the plan to someone in the leadership of the government. It was very hard because Russian leaders changed more often. But then they found the most powerful man in the Russian government who worked just below the elected leaders. He had the power and ability to influence whoever was the leader at the time. The three of them worked two more years finalizing the plans. They knew then that it would take many more years before the plan could be executed." John paused then spoke again. "In the beginning there were only four people—three Chinese and a Russian-- who knew what the plan was. Two more Russians were added, making it six people in all—three Chinese and three Russians-- working to make it happen. These six people, working with the leaders of each government, put the plan into motion."

John paused again to let Brad absorb the information, then continued, "The border wars that you saw between the Russians and us were not real, but only a handful of people knew that. Generals managed the armies, believed what they saw, and operated by the instructions they received from the government. The wars provided each country the opportunity to build up their military without others being suspicious. Also, it provided the reasoning for America to do all she could to help us. We received the best training from Americans, their newest weapons, and most all of their military secrets. Both countries had been spying on all of America's secrets and internet programming to shut down power, water, and phones. For years we probed and tested military secrets. All the Russians had to do was to build a new secret fleet of submarines. These were bigger and more lethal than anyone had seen before. They were designed to carry hundreds of new cruise missile-like rockets. The Russians made cruise missiles like the American ones, but we, the Chinese, developed the way to make them fly low and fast like a rocket. Much of that technology we stole from America."

John paused again, watching Brad as he spoke. "The Russians were so poor we had to secretly loan them most of the money. Because Americans believed there was to be a big war between China and Russia, we could ask them for every type of military ship and aircraft they could spare. They gave us the newest and best they had, and what they would not give us, we bought. We bought up all of the private ammo and gun supplies we could find, knowing it was important to get as many arms out of the hands of the people as possible. We all knew that was the day of the attack, and if we were to have any chance at all, we would have to take out more than half of all American military and all of its Air Force east of the Rockies. We worked hard to have a meeting of all of America's leading military generals and strategists at the Pentagon that morning. To get the meeting, we would have to also sacrifice six of our generals and thirty-five other military men to be there in the Pentagon on that day. We and the Russians had over 8,000 spies ready to take out power, water, internet, and phones if we had to. However, none of them knew the plan. They only needed to stand by to take orders."

"On the second day of the assault, the Chinese government offered to help America against her enemy, and of course the Americans were eager for all the Chinese to come and help them. America understood in the first week that her military had been devastated and that they desperately needed our help. On the first day of the attack there were no more than eight people in each country who knew what the plan was. When all the submarines left Russia, every captain and crew believed they were going to the south coast of China and only one week before, they would receive orders as to where each submarine was to go off the coast of America. They also had been given information to reset each crew's missiles to new targets."

"The plan called for every commercial airplane to be forced to the west so when they were asked, they could be used to move Chinese troops to America sooner and faster. Even the Chinese military generals still believed they were coming to America to fight the Russians who were their enemy also. They were only told of the change in plans on the morning of the day of the surrender."

Brad looked at John, trying to take in and understand all he had just been told. "Why did the American government surrender?" Brad asked.

John studied Brad a moment, knowing he was now going to reveal even more secret information. Then he said, "We had asked that every government figure be in one place so that they could be informed firsthand what the plan of attack was going to be. When they were there, we showed them where all of the U.S. Military was located. Next we showed them where all of the Russian armies had stopped and were located. There was a line running north to south at the east side of North Dakota, Nebraska, Kansas, and Oklahoma. To the east of it, the three Russian armies were arrayed in front of the American armies and the Russians were unloading troops along the Texas Gulf Coast. The American Armies, just to the west of this line, were well-organized and ready to meet the Russian armies. They were located from Montana south to Texas, but since the attack, America only had three small units and were counting on the Chinese. Right behind and to the west of the American armies were three large, well-equipped Chinese armies that were located along US 25 from El Paso to Denver and north to Billings, Montana. There were other Chinese armies scattered out among military bases to the west of the Rockies. Everyone was shown a large map as to the locations of all the military at that moment. The building they were in was completely surrounded and secured. The American government was then told that the plan was that Russia and China intended to attack all American military early the next day. Everyone could see there was no way out. The American military would be completely destroyed in days and they would have to surrender. If not, one by one all the major cities would be destroyed by the Russian subs which were now off the West Coast. They were told that no one would leave the building alive if they did not sign the declaration of surrender on public television. They were also told that after they surrendered, they and their families would be allowed to live out their lives in peace. They had no choice but to surrender and they knew it."

Brad felt disheartened but asked John, "Where are they now?"

"All of them and their families are safely on the island of Guam in the middle of the Pacific Ocean where they will live out the rest of their lives."

Brad looked across the big room where all the people were busily working and tried hard to take in the things he had just heard. The things John had told him flooded across his mind. John knew Brad would need time to absorb what he had just learned. Then Brad turned to John and asked, "Was it necessary to put the whole world into a financial depression?"

John replied, "Remember I said that the one who had conceived the plan loved America even more than his own home land? He wanted to save America, her people, and her great cities. But because America was so financially weak and so in debt, she collapsed. We had never planned nor expected that to happen. Perhaps that was the price that had to be paid to save her. America is strong and we all believed she would never collapse."

Brad did not like what had happened to his nation, though these things often happened in the world to other

countries. But how could they know it would happen to America? Brad sat taking in the news he had been given. A thought suddenly occurred and he had to ask, "When we met years ago, did you already know this was the plan and that it was going to happen soon?"

John paused a moment, then said, "Yes. Everything that has happened, I knew was the plan. What I had not known was what you would tell me about the Lord's faithful few who made up His Church. Maybe it was God's providence, I don't know, that I would meet you and become one of you--a Christian. But then I knew I had to do something to change the plans. This would have been very dangerous for me even to suggest anything like that at that time. It was my responsibility, along with an agent from Russia, to work within the main plan to deal with the population control once we were in America. I prayed and prayed for wisdom to help me find a way to keep some very bad things from happening to the Lord's Church. I prayed for wisdom and God's providential care that something, somehow, someway, could be done to preserve His people."

Brad interrupted John. "Why was it necessary to round up and confine Christians in the camps as you did?"

John explained, "First, anyone who was not a citizen of America would be deported and all people who were in jails or prisons with two or more years remaining on their sentences would be sent to China or Russia to serve out their time in work camps and factories. The original plan called for deportation or killing off those the planners believed to be troublemakers. Since all religious people were considered to be troublemakers, the plan called for all the Jews to be deported and delivered to Israel, all Muslims and middle-eastern people were to be sent to the Muslim country of their choice, and all people who called themselves Christians would be allowed to stay here, but would be made second class citizens, never able to receive benefits or jobs with the government, no higher education, and never the best jobs. All of the best of these things would go to Russian and Chinese citizens or any Americans who did not believe in a God, or had no religion. The plan would make it very hard on the faithful Christian. There would only be a few Christian groups allowed to register for the ability to worship easily."

Brad interrupted, "How was it changed so that it turned out like it is today?"

"Remember, I had just become a part of the planning group only two years before I met you. By the time we met, our plans were finalized. It was myself and a man from Russia who were to design the population control plans for the group, and we finished the plans just before we met. When I became a Christian I knew the plan needed to be changed. There had to be some way to find and separate what I understood to be faithful Christians, and there needed to be a way to keep them safe. I knew then that I needed a way to make the others think that we, the U.S.C., had plans to use this group or to kill them off. But how this was to be done, I did not know. We were only two years away from the target date. It would be very dangerous if the leadership planners saw me as weak or a problem to them. They would simply kill me off and get someone else. I knew I had to do something to save the Christians.

"When I became a Christian, I told my mother. She kept it quiet out of love for her son, but somehow I knew I had to go to her and tell her that I had a problem and needed her wisdom to help me solve it. She did not know about the plan or my involvement in it. I felt a strong urge to tell her that I was very troubled over a decision I had to make. She said to me, 'I don't know how to help you, but I know someone who I would turn to if I were looking for good advice.' She convinced me to speak to this person who might help me with my decision. I did not feel comfortable speaking to a stranger, but my mother was never wrong. She would only say to me that he was a very close friend of our family and that it would be very safe for me to speak with him if he were willing. I thought this might be the most foolish thing I've ever done but I knew I had no other choice.

"A few days later my mother came to me and gave me written instructions as to where and when I was going to be able to meet with this person. All I could think about was how

dangerous it was for me if anyone found out. It kept coming back to me that I had no choice. I must find a way to save the Christians, even at the risk to my own life. I also knew my mother would not send me into danger.

"On the specified day I went where the instructions sent me, along the sea coast at a small, almost-empty fishing village. When I arrived there I could see a single person fishing near the end of the pier. As I made my way down the pier, I turned and looked around several times to see if anyone was following me. When I came close to the person, he told me to keep walking, stop at the end of the pier and look out into the ocean. He was on my left a few feet away. The wind and the sound of the ocean made it difficult for us to hear each other, but then I realized neither would anyone else hear us.

"A voice from a face I could not see said to me, 'Young man, are you on the pier fishing for answers?' I answered, 'Yes, sir. Somehow I must do a good thing, but I do not understand how.' He said, 'I am a good friend of your mother's. What is your dilemma?' Without saying or telling anything I shouldn't, I simply said, 'I have information that I believe is important to know, but I do not know how to approach a very important person with the information.' He asked me, 'What is this information?' I replied, 'I cannot tell you. I am only asking how can I reach someone who is very high above me in reputation, stature, and power?' The man said, 'Who is this person?' I replied, 'I cannot say who he is.' He replied, 'Well, you are not giving me information to help you.' At that he picked up his fishing box and pole, and with his back to me said, 'Tell your mother it is time.' And he walked away. I never turned to see where the man went. I just stood at the end of the pier thinking to myself, 'What have I done? Did I say too much? What did he know that I didn't?' I thought perhaps I had signed my death warrant. Only time would tell. But the man had also given me no answers.

"Two days later, when I returned home, I went to see my mother. She was in the garden behind her home, a place where my sister and I used to run and play as children. She greeted me and asked, 'Did you see him?' I said, 'Yes.' She asked 'Will he help you?' I told her that I did not believe he could help me. She said, 'Let us wait and see.' Then I turned to my mother and said, 'The man told me to tell my mother 'that it is time.' What did that mean?' My mother turned her face away from me. Then she stood and walked over to a small bench in the middle of her garden where she would often sit to meditate and think. I knew she did not want to tell me something. I asked if there was something wrong. For a moment she sat in silence. Then she replied, 'I knew someday I would tell you, but I did not think it would be today.'"

"She stopped, took in a deep breath, then let it out slowly before she continued. 'When your sister was three years old, your father died on the fishing boat that sunk in a storm. After the funeral my cousin, Su Lee, and her husband remained with us for several days. After they left, I began to tell people that I was three months with child and I thought it would be a boy in remembrance of his father. I would fix under my clothes so that all who could see me could tell that I was with child. In the eighth month, I told everyone that I was going to my mother's home in the mountains to have the child. Su Lee, who was also eight months with child, was living nearby. When her child was born, it was reported to the government that the child was aborted before birth and that my new son was born. You remember your aunt Su Lee, who for many years until her death would come and visit and help me take care of you and your sister. Your aunt and uncle secretly saw to all of our needs and have to this day. It was your uncle that saw to it that you got into the military, that you went to college in America, and then received your job in the government.' She looked up at me and said, 'The man you saw on the pier is your father, not your uncle.' I asked her, 'Why didn't he tell me that?' She said, 'Because he was high up in the government and had it been known that he had three children and had broken the law of the land, which states you can have only two children, it would not go well, even for him. It was a law that most people hate. He has always been a good father to you from afar.'"

"Two weeks later I was to attend the meeting of all of the

planning people in a small town outside of Paris, France. There were now about 50 people who were involved in our meetings. There were still only a handful of these people from China who knew the entire plan. Myself and others only knew our part of the plan, and only one or two of us at a time would meet with one or two from the Chinese group and the Russian group. We all knew them and thought of them as the master planners. When it was time for my Russian counterpart and I to meet with them and review our part of the plan, there were two men, one from China and one from Russia who were present that day. These two were considered to be the two master planners. The Russian asked my counterpart if all was ready according to the plan. The Chinese planner asked me if there was any possibility of any last minute changes. My counterpart said no, but I said that I had some late information that would be good for us to consider and that could easily change. We were told to go and come back the next day with any changes to our part of the plan."

"By God's providence I now had been given a way to adjust the plan to save these true Christians. When the Russian and I met to work out my changes to the population control plan, he did not at all like the idea of me having another group of people set aside for China's purposes. He did not want us to have something the Russians did not. So, late into the night, after his second bottle of vodka, I got him to agree that there would be two new groups. There would be one that we wanted and one they wanted. We would both collect and then trade them. China would collect these special Christians and Russia would collect homosexuals. They would be gathered from both countries."

Brad said, "I don't understand. Why did he select homosexuals instead of a religious group?"

"I don't know," John said. "Somewhere in the night he said that he had to have a group of people and those would work well in the Russian labor camps." He looked at the large digital clock on the wall and said, "So that's how it all came about."

Brad felt overwhelmed with the knowledge of all that had gone on in the planning of the takeover of America. He had no more to say or ask. He had only to learn to live with the reality of what had happened.

John shifted in his chair and changed the subject. "There is a big banquet planned for tonight. The president of all China will be present to speak to us. There will be other leaders from Russia and China and all of the state governors and military commanders from each nation. I would like you and Carol to come as my guests with Mary and I."

Brad thought for a moment then asked, "Why me?"

"Because I believe it will be important for you to be there, and for the Church to be represented there."

Later that evening Brad and Carol accompanied John and Mary in a military helicopter to a secret location near the mountains east of San Francisco. As the helicopter approached the resort, Brad saw it was heavily armed with more military security than he had ever seen in one place at any time. Upon landing, they were driven to a large banquet hall. Most of the people were still outside drinking and visiting with each other while waiting for the set time for dinner and the speakers. Brad surveyed the group and estimated that well over 1,500 people were in attendance. From what John had told him, and what he could see, the group was made up of high-ranking U.S.C. and U.S.R. military leaders, governors and their wives, generals and high-ranking officers from both countries, and countless other state government officials.

The four of them made their way through the crowd. John would stop and introduce the other three to governors and military leaders he saw along the way.

As they approached a man who was talking with some Russian military officers, John leaned towards Brad and said, "Remember I told you about my Russian counterpart?"

John stopped next to him and when the Russian saw

John, he smiled and said, "Comrade! It is good to see you here tonight!" He gave John a hearty embrace and asked, "Comrade, are your plans going well?"

"Very well," John replied as he gestured to his wife. "This is my wife, Mary."

The Russian took her hand, nodded his head, and said, "John, you have a beautiful wife. I am delighted to meet her." Then John turned to Brad and Carol. "These are two of my good friends, Brad Wilson and his wife, Carol." John gestured towards the Russian. "This is Zachar Polasky. We have been working on a project together for a few years."

Zachar smiled in such a way that indicated he had already drunk too many vodkas. "Any friend of John is a friend of mine," he said as he snapped to attention before shaking hands with Brad. He also shook hands with Carol. "Another beautiful woman," he said with a broader smile.

At that moment a young Chinese officer came up to John and spoke quietly to him. John turned and said to the others, "We need to go."

They quickly made their way through the crowd to the banquet room doors. There were security soldiers checking everyone before they were allowed to go inside. Everyone except John was checked. Brad noticed and wondered why.

Inside the building they followed the young officer across the large banquet room. John said to Brad, "The vice chairman of all the U.S.C. and the military has asked to see us." John paused as he walked a couple of steps. "Remember, I told you of the man who loved America and conceived the plan? He is the man we are going to see." They came to a door with two heavily-armed Chinese soldiers. The young officer opened the door and directed the four to go inside. When they were in the room, he closed the door behind them.

An older, distinguished-looking man sat with a drink in one hand and paper in the other, reading as he sipped. When the four entered the room, the man set down his drink and papers, and rose to meet them. He wore a dress uniform with four stars on each shoulder and two gold braids around the end of each sleeve. There were six medals pinned on his chest. He had light gray hair and looked to be in his 60s.

When they reached him, John bowed and said, "Sir, this is my wife, Mary, and these are our American friends, Brad and Carol." The man stood quietly, looking at each one in turn. With a smile he said to Mary, "I have heard of you, but I believe this is the first time I have met you."

Mary, too, bowed slightly and said, "Yes, sir, I do believe we have never met before."

He took her hand and said, "I am very thankful to meet you now." Brad noticed both she and John seemed somewhat surprised by the warm greeting. The man asked, "Is it true you have a son?"

John replied, "Yes, we do. His name is John. He is three years old."

The officer said, "Maybe I can see him some day." Then the officer turned and looked at Brad and Carol. "I owe you both a great deal of gratitude for saving the life of my only son."

John was clearly astounded, for no man in his life had ever called him his son.

The officer knew he had caught John off guard. He turned to him and said, "I believe it was you on the pier that day who was fishing for answers."

The officer didn't wait for a response from John, but turned back to Brad and Carol and said, "I understand you are some kind of Christian."

"Yes, sir," Brad answered without hesitation.

"Is it true your God wants you to care for your neighbor?"

"Yes, sir."

"To do good even to those who may mistreat you?"

"Yes, sir."

"And you believe all people are equal?"

"Yes, sir."

"And you are to show respect to all who have authority over you and to follow the laws of your government?"

Brad was amazed the man knew these things and he replied, "Yes, sir. We must love God and His Son first. Then we must do all the things you have mentioned."

John's father looked at them and said, "If all citizens of this great country were to be like you, this would truly be the greatest nation on earth."

The door opened and the young officer said, "Sir, it is time."

John's father nodded his head then turned to his son. "Tonight, our President has come here to appoint me Vice President of the U.S.C. I intend to announce that you will be my second-in-command. You, too, will have authority over the people of this great nation." Then he turned and walked out of the room.

THE END

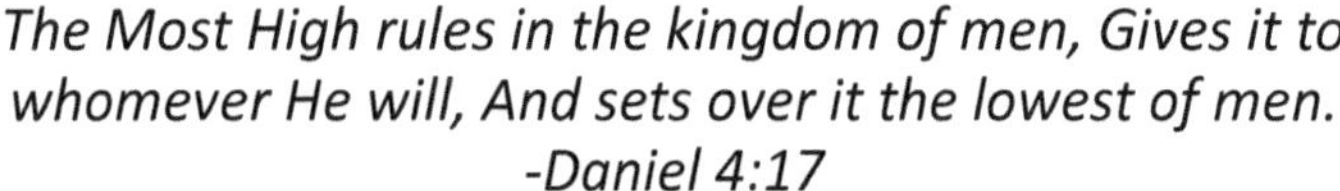

The Most High rules in the kingdom of men, Gives it to whomever He will, And sets over it the lowest of men.
-Daniel 4:17

EPILOGUE

THE SAVED PEOPLE

For over two hundred years America was known as the greatest nation on earth and God had blessed her for His purposes. He had used America to help poor people and nations around the world. God had given America power and opportunity to defeat the evil nations of the world in both World War I, World War II, and others.

Now there would be two nations between the two great oceans where one had been before. One would become great, peaceful, and prosperous. The other would be a place where peace was hard to find, where evil and corrupt men would rule and prosperity would not be found. From time to time there would be disputes between them and their armies would stand up against each other for a time. But they never went to war against each other.

Each state in the two countries would fly its own flag but it was against the law to fly the U.S. flag. The Russian and Chinese military would each fly their national flags. The city of Washington, D.C., where the U.S. government had been, remained walled off and only caretakers were allowed in.

Unexpectedly, the war set off a worldwide depression that would last, in most countries, six to twelve years. But in the U.S. countries it would be eighteen years before economies became stabilized again. China's economy would have its troubles, even at home, but would continue to be the richest economy in the world. Over the next ten years, life expectancy in the two U.S. nations would drop by twenty years.

Wars and rumors of wars would continue to be a part of every nation's history throughout the world. North and South Korea would remain in a continuous war for many years to come, with millions of people in the north dying of hunger each year. The nation of Israel would continue to be at war off and on with her sister countries in the Middle East where thousands would be lost each year due to those conflicts.

From behind the scenes, John's father would pay close attention to how his son treated the people of the land, and how these Christians were allowed their freedom. John's father ruled fifteen years and remained an atheist to his death. John was appointed to take his father's place.

John and Brad remained good friends and brothers in Christ throughout their lifetimes. Brad would work for John in the government, and the two of them would make sure the true Christians of the Lord's Church were free to go wherever they wished to preach and teach the words of Jesus Christ and the good news of His saving love and power. They were also allowed to send missionaries throughout all of China. The government recognized them and gave them special privileges to travel anywhere. They made arrangements for many teachers to be allowed to go into the U.S.R., and Jesus added countless millions to His Church throughout the world. The Lord's Church was free to worship throughout the land and did so on Sundays, the first day of every week.

As Christians lived in peace throughout the nations, all those who rebelled against the military or state governments would be swiftly dealt with, most ending in death. All state government officials and business leaders found guilty of corruption, lying, bribery, or stealing would be swiftly punished, often by death. Those who spoke evil of the authorities would also be swiftly and severely punished. Public punishment was always shown on television and on the internet.

Legal abortion was outlawed in the land. John's father had hated it because it cost him his son.

Satan, the great liar and tempter, would always remain as

king of this earth destroying all the good he could.

Years later Brad said to John, "You have saved the people of Jesus, the Lord's Church in America."

John said, "No, if it had not been for you, I would have not known the truth." John shook his head. "I believe God used you and I together to save His people."

Rulers are not a terror to good works, but to evil. Do you want to be unafraid of the authority? Do what is good, and you will have praise from the same. For he is God's minister to you for good. But if you do evil, be afraid; for he does not bear the sword in vain; for he is God's minister, an avenger to execute wrath on him who practices evil. -Romans 13:3-4

Therefore you must be subject, not only because of wrath but also for conscience' sake. For because of this you also pay taxes, for they are God's ministers attending continually to this very thing. Render therefore to all their due: taxes to whom taxes are due, customs to whom customs, fear to whom fear, honor to whom honor. -Romans 13:5-7

Therefore I exhort first of all that supplications, prayers, intercessions, and giving of thanks be made for all men, for kings and all who are in authority, that we may lead a quiet and peaceable life in all godliness and reverence.
-1 Timothy 2:1-2

Reader's Favorite gives The House a five-star review.

The House by Lacey Deaver is a good Christian story from beginning to end. Cheri is a troubled young woman running for her life. She hides in a truck in Seattle and, after three days without food and water, she escapes from the truck in a small Texas town. Cheri has no money and no place to go, so as she wanders the town she is picked up by the local Sheriff who brings her to the "house" of Margret and Carl Hanna. Daniel is a long time friend of the Hannas and often stays in the guesthouse. Cheri is mean and angry at the recent development in her life. Margret and Daniel befriend her over time and slowly she changes. The strength of growing friendships and belief in God is the crux of this heartwarming story.

The House will make you smile and make you cry, but mostly it will keep you glued to the book until you reach the end. It is a very fast paced story and only took a few hours of reading to finish, but I was really sorry to come to the final page and leave my new friends behind. Lacey Deaver is a marvelous storyteller. She has spiced the book with just enough suspense, drama, romance and uncertainty to keep me reading with great anticipation of the ending. I absolutely adored each of the characters and the plot is flawless. This book is perfect.

-*Reader's Favorite* review   **www.ReadersFavorite.com**

Story by Rudy Cain and book by Lacey Deaver

Book available as e-book on: amazon kindle

Books from wvbs

–Searching for Truth Study Guides–

These study guides, written by **John Moore**, area great resource as a companion to the *Searching for Truth* DVD, or used on their own as a workbook. The material is suitable for individual study or used in any Bible class setting. The text follows the same chapter structure and is nearly a word-for-word transcript of the DVD.

The study guides include extended question sections, including a "Section Review" after each section and a "Chapter Review" at the end of each chapter. To close-out the chapter there is a "Digging Deeper" section, which includes additional verses on the subject matter that are not used in the text. The answer to every question can be found in the Answer Key section at the end of the book. Additionally, six teaching charts are included in the book. These 8.5 x 11 inch, full-color charts cover popular issues such as, "The Book of Daniel & God's Kingdom," "Where do we go when we die?," "Modern Churches Timeline," "The Ten Commandments?," Baptism's significance, and the Church as God's spiritual house.

English Study Guide

Spanish Study Guide

Over 140,000 printed!

Russian

Korean

Swahili

Book available as e-book on: amazon kindle

Reader's Favorite gives Transformed: A Spiritual Journey a four-star review.

Transformed: A Spiritual Journey by Lance Mosher is a profound and inspirational book that documents the important events of the author's life. This spiritual autobiography is peppered with events in life, topics of conversation, and dialogues that speak about the author's emotional and intellectual struggles. The book shows the providence of God and will help readers with open minds to wrestle with themselves and the Lord. The book has spiritual answers to many questions that are already in the minds of readers, and will convince readers about the truths that exist in their beliefs. The book teaches readers to love and respect God, pray regularly, and lead a clean and good life.

The book is uplifting and helpful to all those who want to contemplate the teachings in their lives and the entire essence of their existence. The author's simple and succinct style makes it easy for readers to connect with what he is trying to convey. The author pulls readers into his world and many of his experiences are relatable. The book helps transform many readers, where the truth will set them free instead of debates, opinions or speculations.

God's presence is again reiterated through the author's words and he does an excellent job by helping readers understrand Jesus Christ. This thought provoking book is definitely a good guide for all those readers who are trying to understrand the Bible and the Lord in a better way.

-Readers' Favorite review

www.ReadersFavorite.com

Book available as e-book on: amazon kindle